Sugar

SECRETS...

...& Flirting

This book belongs to:
Kesia McLaren
8. Milton   Mossbourne Community Academy

Mel Sparke

Borough: Hackney

Collins

An imprint of HarperCollinsPublishers

Published in Great Britain by Collins in 2000
Collins is an imprint of HarperCollins*Publishers* Ltd
77–85 Fulham Palace Road, Hammersmith, London W6 8JB

The HarperCollins website address is
www.fireandwater.com

9 8 7 6 5 4 3 2 1

Creative consultant: Karen McCombie
Copyright © Sugar 2000. Licensed with TLC.

ISBN 0 00 710103 1

Printed and bound in Great Britain by
Omnia Books Limited, Glasgow

Secrets...
& Flirting

...Plus!

CAN YOU KEEP A SECRET?
TRY OUR FAB QUIZ AT
THE BACK OF THE BOOK

SOME SECRETS ARE JUST TOO GOOD TO KEEP TO YOURSELF!

CHAPTER 1

●●●●●●●●●●●●●●●●●●●●●●●●●●●

LOOKING AFTER THE DETAILS

"What a let-down!" moaned Catrina Osgood, staring at her copy of OK magazine.

"What's a let-down?" asked Maya Joshi, who, until her friend's sudden outburst, had been idly gazing out of the window of the End-of-the-Line café this Monday morning.

"This!" said Cat, nodding at the glossy pages of smiling celebs spread out on the table.

"What about it?" frowned Maya. Sometimes, working out what was going on in Cat's mind took quite a bit of effort.

"Well, it's rubbish this week – it's all women!" Cat exclaimed, flicking dismissively through the pages. "There's absolutely no gorgeous blokes in here!"

"Well, in my opinion, there's no point wasting your energy fancying famous people anyway," Maya shrugged.

"Why not?" frowned Cat.

"Face it – it's not like you're ever going to meet them, never mind go out with them."

Cat sighed theatrically and shook her head. "Maya, you can be *so* negative. Why *couldn't* it happen? I mean, celebs fall in love, just like normal people!"

"Yeah, but they don't tend to fall in love with *normal* people, just other *famous* people!" Maya pointed out.

"Rubbish," muttered Cat grumpily. "It happens all the time. You won't be so smug when you read about me in a few years time, when I'm starring in my own TV show with my lovely pop star husband!"

"Exactly," Maya grinned. "Famous people are only interested in other famous people. I rest my case."

Cat stuck out her tongue at Maya and turned back to her magazine. But she could never shut up for very long. "Is Joe coming in this morning? Or is he working at Central Sounds again?" she asked, gazing across the table enquiringly.

"No, he's doing a few days in Central Sounds this week, but he's not in there today," replied

Maya. "It's his day off and he's gone to meet Meg at the bus station. She's getting the coach back from Brighton."

"Oh, good! Maybe he'll stop moping now!" snorted Cat. "I mean, did you see his face yesterday? You'd think she'd been gone for two months instead of two days!"

Maya smiled to herself. It was true; Joe Gladwin's forlorn expression had practically put Matt off his Sunday morning fry-up the day before – and it took a lot to put Matt Ryan off his food.

"He's got the love bug and he's got it bad," Maya commented. "I don't know *how* he's going to cope once he's in London and she's in Brighton!"

"He'll be one of those soppy guys you hear about that has to phone her every single day..." muttered Cat.

"Oooh, you wouldn't be jealous, would you?" Maya suggested, a wicked smile on her face.

"Jealous of what? Are you trying to say I've got the hots for Joe or something?" said Cat.

"*No*. I mean, You're jealous that *they're* so much in love – and you're single!"

Cat finally flicked her eyes away from the pages of her magazine and gave a little shrug. "Maybe..." she grumbled. "But you can hardly talk, Maya Joshi, since *you're* single too."

"Yes, but that was through choice, remember," Maya pointed out. "I finished with Alex."

"Thank goodness," sighed Cat.

"Thank goodness? What do you mean?" asked Maya, bristling slightly. "Didn't you like him?"

"Alex? Yeah, but that's not the point, is it?"

"Well, what *is* the point?"

"The point *is*," said Cat, flicking a page over with a cracking sound, "with you on your own, it means I'm not the only one out of our closest friends not to be dating. After all, Kerry and Ollie are so inseparable they're practically *married*; Anna and Matt are all cosy-cosy; and all Sonja can talk about is moving in with her precious Owen when she goes off to uni. At least with *you* being single, there are *two* of us losers!"

"Hey – single does *not* mean loser!" protested Maya.

"I know *that*. But you *are* being a bit of a loser if you don't go to your photography class just 'cause you can't face seeing your ex!" said Cat, narrowing her eyes at her friend.

Maya's felt her face burn. It was true – she had been back from holiday for two weeks now and had found fairly pathetic excuses both Wednesdays not to turn up to the photography club that her ex, Alex McKay, ran. Although she'd spoken to Alex on the phone right after her holiday – and cleared the air over their break-up – she still couldn't quite summon up enough courage to see him face-to-face.

There was only one thing she could do. Change the subject.

"Anyway, why are you so interested in where Joe is today?"

As she spoke, Maya reached out and moved the vase in the middle of the table over to the window, so she could see her friend better. The vase, and the three large plastic flowers in it, was just one of the new innovations that Cyndi – café owner Nick Stanton's new wife – had made around the place. Every table had a similar decoration, much to the bemusement of the workmen who regularly came in for their fry-ups in the mornings.

Maya had been pretty amazed by the number of changes that had taken place since she'd returned from her holiday. Finding that bachelor bloke Nick had got himself married out in America was the biggest shock of all.

"Well, I was just wondering how Joe got on last night – it must be scary looking for somewhere to live in a big place like London," Cat replied to Maya's question.

Maya raised an eyebrow slightly at her friend. It seemed very unlike Cat to be so concerned and interested in the details of Joe's life. Much as everyone in the crowd loved Cat, they knew only too well that her favourite topic of conversation was always herself.

"I hope he got on better than he did on Friday and Saturday," Maya replied cautiously, eyeing Cat up and wondering what her angle was. "He phoned loads of different flats and houses and had no luck with any of them."

"Well, I really, *really* hope he's got something fixed up. And in a cool area too..."

Maya was by now seriously confused. This concern of Cat's was well beyond the call of duty.

"...because," Cat continued, "the first weekend I can afford it, I'm going to be straight down there staying with him. And I'm telling you now – he'd better not expect me to come and visit him if he's living in grotsville!"

Ahh! Maya grinned to herself. *So that's it – Cat sees Joe as her passport to life in the big city!*

London... a career on TV... a celebrity boyfriend... it was all part of Cat's star-spangled vision of her future.

"And he'd better not end up sharing with girls!"

"Why not?" laughed Maya. "In case it drives Meg wild with jealousy?"

"No!" exclaimed Cat. "Because I want him to

be sharing with a bunch of gorgeous boys – so I can get myself a lovely student boyfriend!"

"I thought you said you wanted a celebrity boyfriend?" teased Maya.

"Of course! Doesn't everyone if they have a choice?!" said Cat, wide-eyed. "But until I can get my hands on one, a fit student will do nicely!"

"Cat!" laughed Maya. "Do you think of anything else except—"

"Wow – look at *her*!" Cat interrupted, tapping her finger on a photo, one of a page of celebrities caught on camera while attending a variety of glitzy events. "How ridiculous is that dress?!"

Maya knew she was meant to be horrified by the wispy bits of chiffon ribbons that were barely covering Jennifer Aniston's bits on the pages of *OK*. But, to be honest, she'd seen Cat wear outfits that were almost as revealing (even if they didn't have an exclusive tag on them).

The other reason Maya was finding it hard to concentrate on the photo was that her eyes were being magnetically drawn to the finger that was tapping beside it. The nail extensions that Cat was wearing today were outrageously long, painted electric blue with silver metallic tips and a tiny fake diamond placed dead centre on each talon. It looked like her friend was doing some Beauty

Therapy course homework on herself, even though it was still the holidays.

"Oh, do you like them?" asked Cat, spotting Maya's stare and wiggling all ten fingers around.

The effect was pretty overpowering.

"Cat, how do you manage to *do* anything with those?" asked Maya, practical and to the point as usual.

"What do you mean?" frowned Cat, slightly hurt at the lack of compliments coming her way.

"Like... like going to the loo!" said Maya bluntly. "I mean, how do you even undo your trousers?"

"Carefully..." Cat replied with a casual shrug.

"Gee, those nails are real pretty! Where did you get them done?"

Both Cat and Maya spun round at the sound of Cyndi's syrupy southern American drawl.

"I did them myself!" said Cat proudly, wiggling her fingers in the air for all to see.

"Hey, could you do my nails for me sometime?" asked Cyndi enthusiastically.

"Yeah, sure!" smiled Cat, lapping up the compliment.

"I sure would like something like that in a nice ice pink!" Cyndi continued, leaning her weight on the table and gazing admiringly at Cat's handiwork.

"Well, that would be no problem," gushed Cat. "I've got plenty—"

Just as Cat was about to give an inventory of her nail varnish collection, the public phone began to ring on the other side of the busy café.

"Anna!" yelled Cyndi, turning her blonde head of curls and scanning the room as she settled herself down in the booth next to Cat. "Get that, would you, hon!"

Maya gazed over at a flummoxed-looking Anna, who was struggling to keep her piled-high tray of dirty plates upright, while two small children – ignored by their chatting mothers – crashed into her legs.

"Uh, Cyndi – I've kind of got my hands full!" Anna called over, trying to stop the toddlers thumping each other with her one free hand.

"Well, I'm kind of busy too, hon!" Cyndi called back, tucking her order pad into the pocket of her faded denim shirt. It looked like she definitely considered herself on a break.

Anna, her face like stone, clattered the tray down on the table nearest her, startling the gossiping mums long enough to realise their kids were tearing chunks out of each other. Maya watched Anna stomp over to the phone, wiping her hand on her apron before she picked up the receiver.

"It's one of the things I really miss from back home," smiled Cyndi, spreading her fingers out on the red Formica. "I always went to this cute little beauty salon once a week to get my hair and nails fixed. An' I don't want Nick to get the idea that just 'cause I've landed my man, I'm gonna let myself go!"

"Nick's *not* going to think that!" Cat pointed out. "You had a whirlwind romance! He brought you all the way back from the US to be with him! He's not going to divorce you if you don't have your nails done every week!"

"Now, that's where you're wrong! It's the little details that count in a relationship!" said Cyndi with a knowing look.

"What do you mean?" Cat frowned at her.

"Well, ladies, I hope y'all don't think I was listening in," Cyndi began, "but I couldn't help hearing that you two were talkin' about being single. And if I can give you one piece of advice, it's always to remember the details. That's the way you land yourself a man – an' that's the way you keep him too!"

Maya felt her mouth drop open slightly. She wasn't really up for being told how to land herself a man, but Cat was nodding enthusiastically. Now she understood where Cyndi was coming from she was in total agreement. As far as Cat was concerned, life was about looking good. She couldn't wait to hear more.

"What *kind* of details, Cyndi?"

"Just keepin' yourself pretty, y'know? Nice hair, nice nails, pretty lipstick. It all helps you feel special and a man appreciates a woman takin' good care of herself!"

Maya gave herself a little shake, just to check she hadn't fallen asleep. She could almost believe she was dreaming that she was in some previous millennium, where women stayed at home raising the kids while the cavemen went out and bashed antelope over the head for tea.

"Cyndi – didn't you hear me calling?" It was Anna, who was now standing over their table.

"No, I didn't, honey – I was too busy talking to these ladies!" Cyndi smiled up at Anna.

"The phone – it's for you," Anna replied, her hands on her hips. "It's Nick calling from the cash and carry."

"Oh, my sweet pea!" gushed Cyndi, unnecessarily patting her hair into shape before she dashed over to the phone. "'Scuse me, ladies!"

"Sweet pea?!" Cat and Maya mouthed silently at each other. It wasn't the *first* nickname they'd have thought of for the ponytailed, beer-bellied café owner, much as they liked him.

As soon as Cyndi was out of earshot, Anna took a deep breath, sighed and rolled her eyes.

"Problems?" asked Maya quietly.

"You bet," said Anna, raising an eyebrow. "She's driving me completely mad! I tell you, I've really, honestly been trying to get along with her, but Cyndi's just making my job ten times harder. She keeps making all these changes around here without telling me *and* she orders me about like she owns the place!"

"Well, she is married to the guy that owns it, I suppose," Cat pointed out unhelpfully.

Maya shot her a look across the table and shoved *OK* back under her friend's nose. "Cat, if you can't say anything useful then get back to your magazine!" she snapped. Go on, Anna..."

"It's just that Cyndi's always—"

"Oh, wow! Omigod!" shrieked Cat suddenly.

"What?" asked her two friends, wondering what had got into her.

"Look!" gasped Cat, holding up the magazine.

"What?" the girls repeated, staring at the vaguely familiar face beaming at them from the page.

"It's Ben Fitzpatrick! You know – that really cute British actor who's supposed to be the next big thing?" Cat tried to explain, in the light of Maya and Anna's blank looks.

"Yeah, so... cute pictures of a cute guy. So what?" quizzed Maya.

"It says here that he's *only* doing a new TV drama and he's *only* filming part of it here in Winstead!" Cat practically squealed.

She stared up at the only moderately interested looks on the other girls' faces. "Well, *I* think it's exciting," she huffed. "He's *soooo* gorgeous!"

She turned the magazine back round and planted a huge kiss on Ben Fitzpatrick's smiling face, smudging her pink tinted lipgloss as she did so.

"Here you go..." said Maya, sliding a paper napkin across the table towards Cat.

"What's that for?" Cat frowned.

"Your lipstick's halfway down your chin," grinned Maya. "And you'll never stand a chance with a TV star like him if you don't look after the details!"

"Very funny!" said Cat sarcastically.

"What this about 'details'? What's the joke?" asked Anna.

"Don't ask!" Maya smiled up at her. "You really *don't* want to hear, trust me!"

CHAPTER 2

• •

LOVE IS BLIND

"Anna – can you give me a hand bringing the boxes in from the car?"

Anna wiped her hands on her apron and nodded to Nick who was hovering just outside the back door of the kitchen. "Of course," she said, following him outside into the yard and down the alleyway at the side of the building.

Of course she'd help. Ollie had the day off and it wasn't as if pensioners Irene or Dorothy – the End's catering stalwarts – could be expected to lift heavy boxes from the cash and carry. But what *did* rile Anna slightly was the fact that Nick never thought to ask Cyndi to help out with any of the drearier tasks around the café since she'd arrived.

Maybe he's scared she'll break a fingernail...

Anna thought grumpily as she watched Nick unlock the boot of his car. Glancing back at the café, Anna caught sight of the new Mrs Stanton in the window, standing on a red banquette on tiptoe while she reached up and fiddled with a lacy net curtain that she seemed to be fixing up at the window.

Cyndi, suddenly spotting Anna and Nick out on the pavement, gave a little wave and smile then carried on with perfecting her curtain hanging.

Good to know she's got her priorities right! thought Anna, noticing that Nick's wife hadn't considered that perhaps it might be an idea to come out to lend a hand.

"There you go, Anna!" said Nick brightly, handing Anna a weighty cardboard box.

"Ooof! OK, I've got it..." mumbled Anna. Then – despite the fact that she knew her arm muscles would hate her for it later – Anna paused. Now was as good a chance as any to bring up the problem of Cyndi and her role at the café.

"Nick – can I ask you something?" she began, trying to work out how to handle the situation tactfully.

"Yep?" said Nick, turning to face her.

Anna squinted for a second. There was something different about Nick, but she couldn't quite work out what it was. Then it dawned on her – it was the first time she'd ever seen her boss so neat and clean-shaven. It looked as if Cyndi was definitely up for smoothing the edges off her rough diamond.

"Um, it's just the situation with Cyndi really," Anna dived in, remembering what she was trying to say. "I mean, is she in charge? Over me and Ollie and everyone?"

"Cyndi? No! Of course not!" Nick grinned broadly in surprise. "She's not even officially working in the café – she's not allowed to, till we get all the mess with immigration sorted! It's so great, her lending a hand like this..."

Anna remembered somewhere in the surprise of those first few days after her boss had arrived home that Nick had explained to everyone that since Cyndi was technically over in Britain on a holiday visa, she wouldn't be able to have a job. But she would at least be able to help around the End, in an unpaid kind of way. Only, as Anna was discovering, Cyndi's help was turning out to be more of a hindrance.

"Nick – I don't mean to be funny or anything – but there've been a lot of changes going on. The thing is, I don't feel fully in the picture which is making it hard to do my job properly," Anna continued, picking her words carefully as she hoisted her box further up in her arms and rested a corner of it on the roof of the car.

"What changes? Like the curtains?" Nick frowned in puzzlement. "I know I'm a bloke, but I thought they looked kind of nice."

"It's not the nets," Anna shook her head, staggering under her load as she followed Nick along the alleyway. "It's lots of other stuff too!"

Nick turned round and the hurt puppy dog expression he was wearing reminded Anna fleetingly of Ollie, revealing a previously concealed family resemblance. *Though Nick looks more like a battered old hound dog,* Anna amended her mental image.

At the same moment, Anna realised that complaining was pointless. Nick had met Cyndi on holiday, fallen in love with her, travelled out to see her again, run off to Las Vegas and got married in a chapel playing Elvis songs, then whisked her back across the ocean. It was fair to say he was besotted. Right now, Nick was so in love that he couldn't take even the slightest criticism of his new wife.

"Oh, look – it's nothing really," Anna found herself backtracking. "Forget I ever said—" She didn't get a chance to finish her sentence.

"Sweetie pie!" grinned Cyndi, appearing in the

doorway of the kitchen as they approached it. "Did you get those cute little serviettes from the store?"

"Yes – these are the right ones, aren't they?" Nick replied bashfully, holding up a clear cellophane package.

"That's right, sugar – the ones with the darlin' little red roses!" Cyndi exclaimed, grabbing the package excitedly.

Anna winced, and it wasn't just from the weight of the box she was carrying. She'd just had another vision – that of several burly workmen wiping egg from their mouths with tiny floral paper napkins...

God, love can be scary! thought Anna as she watched Cyndi and Nick smooching over the serviettes. *'Specially when it turns your brain to mush!*

CHAPTER 3

●●●●●●●●●●●●●●●●●●●●●●●●●●●

OLLIE FACES FACTS

"Do you guys want to come up to the flat? There's a brilliant rock documentary starting on MTV in about ten minutes," said Ollie, checking his watch.

It was Tuesday night and the four members of The Loud – Ollie, Joe, Billy and Andy – had just finished their regular rehearsal in the back room of The Swan, Ollie's parents' pub.

"Can't. Busy tonight," said Billy Sanderson, clipping his guitar case closed.

"Hey, hey!" laughed Ollie. "A hot date, eh? Don't tell me you've stopped just *flirting* with Gaby and *finally* got round to asking her out!"

Gabrielle Adjani – an ex-girlfriend of Matt's – had worked a few shifts at the End-of-the-Line café while Nick took off to America. Now that she'd rekindled her friendship with Matt and his crowd, she'd been popping into the End on a regular basis. Billy had soon become smitten – and his mates took great pleasure in teasing him about it.

"Nope, I haven't asked her out yet," Billy grinned broadly. "I haven't plucked up the courage to do that – I'm still too scared Matt might thump me one for going out with his ex!"

Andy and Joe, busy taking apart their own gear, laughed out loud at Billy's typically jokey remark.

"Nope, I'm not taking any chances," Billy continued, still grinning. "I don't want to see Matt's rusty old Lada coming straight at me down a darkened alleyway one night!"

"As if!" chuckled Joe.

"He wouldn't risk damaging his only form of transport," put in Andy wryly.

"Anyway," shrugged Billy, "I'm just taking my time – making sure Gaby's not still hung up on *him*!"

"Nah, I can't see it," said Ollie, shaking his head. "She was cool when she found out he's dating Anna now, wasn't she? That's not a sign of someone who's desperate to get back with her ex, is it?"

"Whatever," shrugged Billy. "I'm just going to take it slowly. There's nothing worse than fancying someone who doesn't fancy you back."

"So," said Ollie, getting back on subject, "if it's

not Gaby you're seeing tonight, who's the hot date?"

"Andy," said Billy, nodding his head in the direction of the skinny bass player, who suddenly gave a hoot of laughter.

"We're going to check out that new action movie at the late show at the Odeon. Y'know – the one with whatsisname in it," Andy King explained to the others. "Either of you two fancy coming?"

"Yeah, go on!" Billy said enthusiastically. "There's supposed to be some amazing special effects!"

"Nah, I can't. I want to watch this telly programme – *and* I promised I'd give my sister a call tonight," Ollie shook his untidy head of dark-blond hair so that it flopped over his eyes.

"Natasha?" said Billy, his eyes automatically lighting up at the mention of Ollie's very pretty twin sister. "Couldn't you phone her tomorrow or something? And tape the TV thing?"

"No, I've got to play the good brother and keep in touch with Tasha – she's been feeling so fragile lately," Ollie explained, plonking himself down on an amp.

"Is she OK now?" asked Andy, frowning in concern.

"Yeah – did she get things sorted out with her agency?" Billy chipped in.

All the friends knew what Ollie's sister had gone through recently. She'd been modelling in Milan for the summer, but had been shocked to find that one rogue booker at her Italian agency had been sending girls to work for clients who expected a lot *more* than just fashion shots. At first, the round of parties she'd been invited to had seemed the usual fun, until she realised that everyone there was either a young, beautiful girl or a sleazy older man – and it didn't take too long for one of these men to let her know exactly what he had in mind.

"Her agency in London was cool," Ollie nodded. "They'd no idea all that stuff was going on, and when the office in Milan found out, the dodgy booker working there was sacked on the spot."

"Who said models have a glamorous life?" Billy commented. "Well, good for Tasha – she obviously did the right thing by getting out of there. But anyway, what about you, Joe? Do you fancy checking out this movie?"

"No thanks," said Joe, shaking his head. "I'm trying to spend as little money as possible right now." He had helped out at the End-of-the-Line café from time to time during the summer, and the last couple of weeks he'd managed to cover a few holiday shifts at Central Sounds, the music shop in town, but things were financially pretty tight for

Joe. He was desperate to save a bit of money prior to his big move to London and university.

"Of course! It's not long till you're off, is it?" said Andy.

"Nope."

"Hey! Look at the time!" exclaimed Billy, glancing at his watch. "C'mon, Andy – we've still got to dump this stuff at your place. We'd better head off now or we'll be stuck in the queue for hours."

"See you guys!" Ollie yelled at their retreating figures as they pushed open the doors that led to the front bar. His words were drowned out by an ear-splitting clatter of cymbals crashing to the floor.

"Got 'em!" said Ollie, grabbing the shiny discs where they'd fallen at his feet and passing them back to Joe to pack away. "Hey, are you OK, Joe? You were pretty quiet tonight..."

Out of all the boys, Joe was always the quiet one, even at the best of times. But Ollie – as his best friend – was the one most qualified to spot when Joe's level of quietness had more to it than usual. Tonight was one of those times.

"I s'pose. Just got stuff on my mind," said Joe, checking his cymbals over for any dents. "Thinking about London, I guess..."

"You're still looking forward to going, you?" Ollie asked warily.

"Oh, university and everything, definitely!" nodded Joe. "It's just that at this rate, I'll be sleeping in my Fiat in the car park!"

"Still no luck finding a flat then?" asked Ollie, helping Joe to finish taking apart his kit.

It wasn't only kindness motivating Ollie to help out. When Joe got distracted, he often got clumsy too – which meant that he could well put his foot through the bass drum. With a gig to play on Thursday, this would be a disaster.

"Nope. I can't find a room anywhere. I dunno what I'm going to do, Ol..." mumbled Joe despondently. "I don't even know why half these places bother to advertise – it seems like they're gone before I can pick up the phone, let alone go down to see anything."

"Hey!" said Ollie cheerfully, reaching over to punch his mate's arm. "It'll work out – it's got to. Something'll turn up!"

Joe looked at Ollie and was tempted to say, "Yeah, like what?" but he knew Ollie was just trying to do his best to sound positive. Not that that was the tiniest bit of help right now.

"Listen, I was thinking about something else too," Joe began, knowing he was about to bring up a subject that neither of them was keen to talk about, even though it was something they couldn't afford to ignore for very much longer.

"What's that then?"

"Ol, I *am* going in three weeks..."

"I know!" laughed Ollie. "That's what we were just talking about!"

"So you're going to have to start looking for another drummer for The Loud," mumbled Joe. "And *soon*..."

The smile faded from Ollie's face as reality sunk in. It was Ollie's worst failing: for all his optimism and good humour, he had a terrible habit of burying his head in the sand when it came to problems. And although Ollie had known about Joe's plans to move to London for ages now, in his mind it was still something that was due to happen way off in the future.

"Yeah... a new drummer! I guess I'd better do something about that!" Ollie said unconvincingly, his eyes wide with surprise – as if it was the first time he'd registered that Joe would actually be leaving Winstead.

"Why don't you put an ad up in Central Sounds? Like we did when we were looking for a guitarist and a bass player? When we found Billy and Andy?" Joe suggested helpfully, knowing that his best mate needed that extra little shove to get him going. Otherwise, The Loud were likely to end up playing at the Railway Tavern with a great big space where the drum kit – and drummer – should have been.

"Good idea – I'll get an ad up on their message board tomorrow," Ollie nodded.

"And what about putting a sign up at the gig on Thursday night?" Joe continued. "There're plenty of people who come along every week to see us. Maybe your new drummer'll be out there in the audience waiting!"

"Yeah, but he's not going to be our *new* drummer, is he?" Ollie contradicted.

"How do you mean?" frowned Joe.

"He'll just be our *temporary* drummer," Ollie spelt out. "We've talked about this before, Joe – you'll always be The Loud's number one. You'll be straight back in whenever you're back for the holidays. This guy will just be filling in – keeping your drum stool warm for you!"

"Sure!" said Joe, grinning broadly.

But deep down inside, Joe *wasn't* so sure. Of course he still wanted to be part of the band – he and Ollie had started the whole thing off together, after all. But the closer the move to London got, the more certain Joe was that his whole life was going to change – forever.

Even if his best mate was burying his head in the sand about that too...

CHAPTER 4

● ●

CAT'S SUPERSONIC SURPRISE

As Kerry Bellamy walked towards the gravel driveway that led to Matt's – and now Cat's – house, she could already hear music blasting out.

But she could tell from the girly pop vocals, as well as the live girly voices singing along, that the sounds didn't have anything to do with Matt. He might be forced to play the likes of Steps at a birthday party he was DJing at, but he definitely wouldn't be caught dead listening to them – at full volume – in his own home. Being the total music snob that he was, off duty Matt only listened to the latest, hippest dance tracks.

Kerry grinned; now that she'd turned into the driveway, she could see Sonja Harvey and Cat lying flat on their backs under the cherry tree, yelling away at the tops of their voices and waving their arms around in time to the music.

"That's the laziest dancing I've ever seen!" she called over to both girls as she strode across the grass to join them.

"Hi, Kez!" Sonja called back, pushing herself up on to her elbows, her honey-blonde hair piled up in a messy topknot.

"What took you so long, Kez?" said Cat, reaching over to lower the volume control on her portable CD player. "We've been here for hours."

"A little thing called work, remember?" Kerry answered, pointing a finger at the white coat-dress that she hadn't had time to change out of as she'd hurried to leave the chemist's and make the most of her Wednesday half day.

Kerry worked every Saturday in Mr Hardy's shop, but for the last couple of weeks she'd been working full-time, covering for staff summer holidays. She would be working there right up until she began teacher training college in the autumn. Kerry was hoping the money she was earning would see her through at least the first term of her course, even though she was going to remain living at home.

"Anyway, what are you two up to?" she asked, looking down at the pile of empty crisp packets and fizzy drink cans scattered on the grass beside the

CD player. "I thought we were on a fitness kick? I thought we were supposed to be playing frisbee this afternoon?"

Lazily, Sonja stretched over and grabbed a luminous plastic disc from beside her. "Ready when you are!" she grinned at Kerry.

"Listen, can I get changed in your room, Cat?" Kerry asked, bending down and rooting around in her bag for her shorts and vest top.

"'Course. As long as you bring more drinks and crisps when you come back out," Cat demanded. "There's a big bag of tortilla chips on top of the fridge!"

"How lazy are you two?" asked Kerry with a smile as she gazed down at her mates. "I've been working *all* morning and you still want me to act as waitress?"

"Oh, but you're so good at it, you could practically get a job at the End..." Cat whined jokingly. Then, suddenly animated, she sat up with quite a different expression. "Kez, *you've* been in town today – you haven't heard any more rumours about where Ben Fitzpatrick is, have you? The local paper said that filming started yesterday, but I can't believe they didn't mention *where*!"

"No," Kerry replied, rolling her eyes. "I haven't heard anything."

Although she hadn't seen Cat in the last couple of days, she'd heard from Maya and Sonja that Ben Fitzpatrick was practically Cat's only topic of conversation right now. Kerry had to agree that he was very tasty to look at, and that it was exciting knowing that a real star and his film crew were somewhere in Winstead.

But Cat was burning up with curiosity to the point of obsession. Kerry could see that, for Cat, it was like one of her favourite celebrity magazine stories coming to life.

"So how come you're lying around here instead of scouring the streets looking for him?" asked Kerry, picking up the empty cans and crisp packets to take inside with her to bin.

"She tried that yesterday," said Sonja, tipping her sunglasses down and staring meaningfully at Kerry over the top of them. "Only trouble was, she wore her new sandals and got ten thousand blisters. *That's* what's stopping her today."

From her reclining position on the blanket spread over the grass, Cat raised both legs up inelegantly, her shorts riding up her bum, so that Kerry could inspect the damage.

"Ouch!" Kerry winced at the sight of the red-rubbed skin and watery bumps on her friend's heels. "No man's worth that much pain, Cat!"

"Well, he would have been – if I'd found him!" Cat moaned, her legs still aloft.

"Wow! Wish I had a camera!" came Matt's voice from nearby, making them all jump.

Cat immediately rolled to a sitting position and stared up at her house-mate.

"What're you on about?!" she snapped, more embarrassed than annoyed.

"Well, once you're a famous TV star – like you're always *saying* you're going to be – I could sell embarrassing snaps of you like that to the tabloids!"

Sonja and Kerry couldn't hide their giggles, even though Cat turned to each of them with don't-encourage-him! glowers.

"What d'you want anyway, Matt?" Cat demanded, lowering her sunglasses on to the bridge of her nose in an attempt to regain her cool.

"I dunno," shrugged Matt. "Maybe I came out here 'cause it's my garden and I'm allowed to."

"Very funny," muttered Cat petulantly as Sonja and Kerry carried on sniggering.

"Or maybe it's because Sonja and Kerry are my friends," Matt continued, "and I felt like saying hello."

"Well, say it and go," Cat said, sticking out her tongue at him.

"Or maybe it's because I'm a genuinely nice guy, Cat, and I just wanted to let you know that Vikki just called on her mobile and says she's on her way here."

Cat fumed – she didn't want to say thank you to Matt, even though she knew she should. Luckily, Vikki Grant helped her out of a grovelling apology by turning into the driveway at that very moment.

"Hey, guys!" she called out, giving them all an enthusiastic wave. Her black plaited hair extensions fanned out behind her as she hurried towards them.

"Hi, Vik! Didn't expect to see you today," shouted Cat. "What's up!"

"Only something brilliant!" said Vikki as she neared them.

"Like?!" asked Cat, whipping off her sunglasses and squinting at her college friend.

"Well!" Vikki exclaimed, slightly breathlessly, "do you guys know Ben Fitzpatrick?"

"Not personally," Matt tried to joke, but his wisecrack was drowned out by Sonja and Kerry's ironic laughter and Cat's ear-piercing squeals.

"Ben Fitzpatrick?!" she squeaked. "Of *course* I know him! He's *here*, filming. Omigod – have you heard where he's staying? Do you know where the action is? Oh, you haven't *seen* him, have you?!"

"Yes, I've heard where he's staying and yes, I

know where the programme's being filmed!" Vikki told her, laughing at her friend's overexcitement.

"EEEEEEEEEEEEK!!!" yelped Cat and the others winced. "Where? Tell me *every*thing!"

"Hold on, hold on!" giggled Vikki. "*That's* not the bit that's brilliant! It's better, much better—"

"What – don't tell me he's got this weird idea that Cat can actually *do* make-up and has asked for her to be his personal face powderer?!" Matt chipped in cheekily.

"Better than that!" gushed Vikki, her eyes twinkling with her secret.

With her hands clasped over her face and mouth, it looked like Cat was about to faint with excitement – so it was probably just as well she was still sitting on the grass.

"Cat," said Vikki, crouching down in front of her friend, "you and me—"

Kerry, Sonja – and even Matt – found themselves holding their breath.

"—are only going to be starring alongside Ben Fitzpatrick in his new show!!"

"AAAAAHHHHHHHEEEEEEEEEEEEEEEEE!"

And with that supersonic shriek emitting from Catrina Osgood, dogs the length and breadth of Winstead jerked to attention and howled in response.

Sonja winced again and then – seeing that her cousin was temporarily speechless – tried to get some facts straightened out.

"But how come?" she quizzed Vikki.

"Well, Jeff Patterson – you know, the Head of English and Drama at college? – he just phoned me!" Vikki explained. "He got a call from the TV people, asking if any of his students fancied being extras!"

"Wow!" said Kerry. Cat was still speechless with shock.

"But he couldn't get hold of lots of people, because of the holidays," Vikki continued. "So it's just going to be three others from my class, plus me and Cat, of course!"

Sonja turned to face Cat again. "Are you OK?" she asked. "Say something!"

Cat looked glazed. "Pass..." she began breathlessly, "the... frisbee..."

"Huh?" frowned Matt. What was going on? Had Cat gone mad? Why did she suddenly want to play a game of frisbee after hearing such amazing news?

Sonja, just as confused, passed over the plastic disc.

"Phew! That's better!" gasped Cat, fanning her burning face with it. "I was sure I was going to faint!"

"Do you want anything else?" asked Kerry, full of concern. "A glass of water?"

"No," Cat shook her head. "Just my mobile..."

"Your mobile? What for?" frowned Sonja.

A wicked smile crept on to Cat's face. "I've got to phone Maya and tell her about this..."

"I don't get it..." said Kerry, sensing there was more to this than keeping Maya up to date with crowd gossip.

"Oh, it's just a conversation we were having the other day," Cat shrugged. "She said that ordinary people virtually never get the chance to meet famous people, let alone go out with them..."

"And, let me guess," grinned Sonja, "you'd like to prove her wrong?"

Cat raised her eyebrows and smiled.

CHAPTER 5

• •

HI! MY NAME IS ANNA!

"Come on now, I wanna see a real big smile, Irene!" Cyndi called out. "And what about a little wave, huh?"

When Matt walked into the End, looking forward to entertaining Anna with Cat's latest news, the first thing he saw was Irene, the elderly waitress, looking flustered. And no wonder: Cyndi had her standing against one white wall of the café and was asking her to turn this way and that, as she pointed and clicked a Polaroid camera at her.

Irene fluffed her grey hair for a second between takes as she tried to ignore the stares of the puzzled customers.

Looking round the café, he spotted Gabrielle and her friend, Sasha, just leaving a nearby table.

"What's going on?" he asked as they walked to the door.

"Apparently, it's Cyndi's new idea," Gaby answered in a low voice, even though the country record twanging away on the jukebox – another of Cyndi's little touches – masked their voices.

"Uh-oh," muttered Matt. "What is it this time?"

"She wants to put a board up on the wall behind the till, with the photos and names of all the staff on it. You know, like they do in places like McDonald's. Only Anna says that Cyndi wants everyone to smile and wave and do 'cute' stuff..."

"Is Anna around?" asked Matt, wondering what his normally calm and sensible girlfriend thought of this latest bird-brained scheme.

"She's on her lunchbreak, upstairs in the flat," Gabrielle told him. "And yeah, she's had her photo taken – we were watching. Don't think she enjoyed it much though!"

"I don't suppose she did!" Matt grinned down conspiratorially at the two girls.

"See you later!" whispered Gaby, slipping out of the door with Sasha in tow.

"Oh, hi Matt, sugar!" trilled Cyndi, suddenly spotting him. "You stopping for somethin' to eat?"

"No, no," replied Matt hastily. "I'm looking for Anna. I heard she's upstairs, so I'll just, er, go on up!"

"Sure thing, honey!" said Cyndi, waving him off with her long pink nails – courtesy of Cat – before she continued pointing her camera at her victim.

As he made his way out into the street again, Matt could just make out Cyndi instructing loudly, "Irene, what about if you just lift your shoulders up and say 'ooh!' like you're doin' 'peekaboo' to the camera. It'll look real cute!"

He dreaded to think what pose she'd asked Anna to do...

• • •

"Like this!" said Anna, sticking a fake, cheesy smile on her face and holding up both thumbs on either side.

"Urghhhhh..." Matt groaned. He flopped down into one of the armchairs in the small flat and put his feet on the coffee table in front of him, disturbing the brightly coloured cards spread all over it. He was too concerned about Anna to pay much attention to them.

"And did you notice the new name badges we've got?" his girlfriend asked as she sat back down on her sofa, grimacing at the mess Matt had made of her cards.

"Nope," he replied. He'd been too busy gawping at Cyndi doing her photography bit to notice whether or not Irene had been wearing a new badge.

"Here, look!" said Anna, picking something up off the edge of the coffee table and passing it over to him. Matt took the white, rectangular plastic badge and read aloud the words printed in pink on it.

Hi! My name is Anna! What can I do for you today?

It was pretty funny, but Matt fought to subdue the hoot of laughter he could feel bubbling up inside. After all, he didn't have to wear it. "Has Ollie seen this yet? I can *really* see him and Nick pinning on one of these with their names spelled out in pink!" he guffawed, trying to sound sympathetic too.

"Oh, yes! Ollie's got his on like a good boy, down in the kitchen. But the boys' names are all printed in *blue* – it's only us girls that have them in *pink*!" Anna explained, rolling her eyes to the ceiling.

"Mmm, nice touch!" joked Matt.

"Oh, but Matt – what's it going to be like, with those stupid photos and these crap badges?" Anna fretted. "How are the customers going to take us seriously? And all the school kids – specially ones like Maya's sarky sister – are never going to stop taking the mick!"

"How come Nick's *going* for all this?" Matt frowned, flipping the name tag in the air towards Anna, expecting her to lean forwards and catch it.

Only she didn't bother. Instead she just let the badge drop to the floor, where it went skittering under the sofa.

"Love!" shrugged Anna. "It's made his brain go soggy!"

"Well, I guess there's nothing wrong with someone being in love, is there?" Matt smiled at her, hoping for a smile in return.

It didn't come.

"I mean, it's nothing too serious, is it?" he continued. "I'm sure everyone'll get used to it."

"But it could get more serious," said Anna ominously.

"How do you figure that one out?"

"Well," said Anna, "we're kind of overstaffed at the moment..."

It took a long time for things to dawn on Matt. But suddenly, he could see what was *really* bothering Anna about Cyndi. It wasn't just stupid name tags and dopey new signs on the loo doors – it was the fact that Anna was scared she was going to lose her job.

"Hey! Don't go thinking Nick will let you go!" Matt assured his girlfriend, joining her on the sofa.

"You're his right-hand woman!" He wrapped a comforting arm around her shoulders and pulled her close.

"But for how much longer?" Anna blinked at him, the worry apparent in her eyes. "I mean, once everything is sorted with the immigration department, Cyndi will be working in the café legitimately. Nick won't need – or be able to afford – to keep me on too!"

"Don't be silly!" Matt tried to laugh, but thinking about it, he could see what she meant. Out of the regular staff, Ollie was unlikely to get the boot, because he was Nick's nephew and had been there longest. And Dorothy and Irene only worked part-time shifts. Out of everyone, it was more likely that Anna would be the one to be made redundant, if it came to it.

"I know it's not the best job in the world, Matt, and it's not like I ever saw myself being a waitress forever, but I don't want to lose it either, not while I'm still trying to figure out what it is I *do* want to do," Anna continued fretting. "And 'specially not since I'd lose my home into the bargain!"

Matt opened and shut his mouth as he realised the significance of what she'd just said. Having the flat above the End thrown in with her job *did* make Anna's situation more complicated.

"I, uh… well, it might not come to that," he said unconvincingly as he struggled to think of something constructive to say. "Anyway, all that immigration stuff can take months and months to sort out. *And*—" He suddenly had a thought.

"And what?" asked Anna.

"And anyway, it was a total whirlwind thing for Nick and Cyndi – I mean, they don't even know each other that well, do they? It's like, he meets her on holiday earlier this year; they keep in touch by phone; he goes back over and marries her?! It's not exactly rock solid, is it? Who knows if they're even going to last!"

"Matt, that's a terrible thing to say!" Anna was visibly shocked. "Anyway, the cards predict they will…" She pointed to the colourful cards that were now scattered over the coffee table. Her boyfriend squinted down at them.

"What are you on about?" he asked her. "What is this stuff?"

"Tarot cards. I bought this set, and a book that explains how to use them, from that new shop on the High Street that sells crystals and things."

"What, you're trying to see into the future?" Matt asked, wondering, not for the first time, how someone as reasonable as Anna could be influenced by things like the position of a few pretty pictures spread on a table.

"Kind of." Anna shrugged, looking a little shy in the face of her boyfriend's obvious scepticism. "It's just that I've been feeling so muddled lately that I thought, why not? If trying to read the cards can help me sort out stuff in my head then it's worth a go..."

"So what are they supposed to say?" said Matt dubiously, twisting his head around to make sense of the images in front of him.

"Well," Anna began to explain, taking up a book that was lying open by her side and studying it and straightening up the cards at the same time, "this row here is meant to represent what's going on around me at the moment..."

Matt looked at the line of cards she was pointing at and could hardly tell them apart. It was all figures and rainbows and suns and moons.

"...and it says that the situation is a happy and solid one – but for others, not for me. Which I reckon means Cyndi and her mad ideas are here to stay."

Matt frowned. Much as he loved Anna, he couldn't really get his head around this stuff.

"And this bit here," Anna continued, pointing to another jumble of cards, "is supposed to be my future. And all these cards mean 'change'. See what I mean?"

"Well, I dunno," shrugged Matt. "But listen, why don't you just try not to worry about it, eh?"

"But Matt, it's hard not to!" Anna protested as her boyfriend pulled her towards him and kissed her.

"Hey, try and ignore it for now, OK?" he tried to reassure her. "Me and you are going out to Ibiza next month; maybe all you really need is to get away for a while and it'll seem better."

Anna gazed up at his handsome face, full of concern. "You're right – I should just try and concentrate on the holiday," she smiled at him. "Look forward to something positive..."

"Too right," said Matt, hugging her close and nuzzling his face into her hair. "And, you never know, things might not work out as badly as you think."

But if anyone ever made me wear a badge that said 'Hi! My name is Matt!', he thought silently to himself, *I'd tell them where to stuff it – and their job!*

CHAPTER 6

• •

DAYDREAMS AND MAKE-OVERS

Ben Fitzpatrick ran his hand over his short crop of
dark hair and sighed.

With his gaze downcast, Cat took the
opportunity to stare at him. He was definitely –
impossibly! – more gorgeous in the flesh than he
was in any of his TV appearances or magazine
photos – and they were cute enough.

Ben had that rough diamond look: handsome,
but not in a pretty, model boy way. With her heart
thumping a little harder than usual, Cat took in his
sexy, sleepy-looking brown eyes, which were
framed by thick, dark brows, à la Liam 'n' Noel. His
broad jaw was moving slightly as he distractedly
chewed gum. Dressed in an old black suede jacket
and dark blue jeans, with just a hint of stubble

round his chin, he reminded Cat of how she'd first seen him – acting as the young guy in a TV series about East End gangsters.

When Ben suddenly sighed again, Cat shuddered. She should say something, she knew. This was her big chance...

"What's up? Can I help?" Cat asked, stepping closer to him, wondering if she should reach out – like she would with any of her boy mates – and put a comforting hand on his shoulder. But, for once in her impulsive life, she didn't dare.

At her words, Ben looked directly into her eyes. Her heart leapt as she saw that his trademark smouldering gaze had turned into a look of tortured longing.

"Yeah, you can help," he said simply, his voice cracking slightly with emotion.

Cat felt dizzy. "How? What do you want me to do?" she replied, finding herself melting in the spotlight of those eyes.

"Say 'yes'," he said earnestly.

"Yes to what?"

A shy smile broke out on Ben's face. "Cat – do you believe in love at first sight?"

Instantly she understood, even though she couldn't trust herself to believe it.

"Yes!" she whispered.

"Good, 'cause I do too," said Ben, moving closer to her. "It's crazy, but the moment I saw you, I just knew you were The One. And I've been trying to work up the courage to tell you..."

"Oh, Ben!" sighed Cat, tilting her head to one side as he gently cupped his hand around her cheek. His fingertips on her skin felt as if they were generating tiny little electric shocks.

"Cat, I've got to ask," he whispered. "Do you feel the same?"

"Yes!" she breathed softly as his beautiful face bent down to kiss her...

"Oi!"

The yell, and the accompanying hammering slaps on the bathroom door, jolted Cat out of her delicious daydream.

"Get a move on, Cat!" she heard Matt bark. "I've got to leave for the Railway Tavern in five minutes and I need to have a shower now!"

Cat pulled her towel tighter around her chest, wiped the steam from the bathroom mirror and stared at her reflection.

Me and Ben Fitzpatrick... I wonder if it could happen for real? she mused, with a shiver of excitement. Tomorrow would be her first day of filming; her first chance to get to know him; to make her daydream come true...

"Cat – move it!" Matt's muffled cry came through the door again.

She turned, flipped the lock and yanked the door open. "Some people haven't got a romantic bone in their body!" she growled at him as she strode past.

Matt frowned as he watched her walk away, padding little wet footprints into the carpet. He had no idea what Cat was on about, but then that wasn't exactly unusual...

● ● ●

"How did your photography club go last night, Maya?" asked Sonja, before taking a big slurp out of her Coke.

The Loud were due to take the stage shortly and, one by one, the girls – including Meg but minus Cat – had arrived at the Railway Tavern and gathered around a table, chatting and catching up with the latest gossip.

"Oh, yeah – it was the first time you'd seen Alex since your holiday," Kerry remembered.

"It was OK," said Maya, wrinkling her nose. It had been totally weird actually, but Maya didn't feel like analysing the details in depth, even with her best friends – it felt too raw. Just seeing this person she'd recently been so close to, and now trying to be polite and friendly in a distant way, had felt strange and uncomfortable. Was this how you were *supposed* to feel? Maya just didn't know.

The strangest moment of all had been when Alex had said, "Glad to have you back at the club – we've missed you." Maya suddenly looked into his grey eyes and realised that she would never again kiss this person or feel his arms wrap themselves around her...

"What about the others?" asked Anna. "Do they know you guys have split up?"

"Yeah, it's filtered through to everyone – thanks to Billy and Andy letting people know – and, to tell you the truth, everyone was really sweet." Maya gave a sad little smile. "Especially Ashleigh."

"Wasn't she the one who gave you a hard time?" asked Sonja. "The one who thought Alex entered your photo for that big competition just 'cause you were his girlfriend?"

"Yes, but she's fine now," Maya shrugged, keen to forget that talk of favouritism. "She even told me last night that she thought my entry was the best out of everyone's at the club, which was really sweet of her. Not that I think I've got a hope of winning..."

"When is the winner going to be announced?" asked Kerry, leaning forward so she could hear the conversation better, now that the pub was filling up and getting noisier.

"Next week sometime, I think. But don't hold your breath – I'm not going to get anywhere with it," Maya laughed, seeing Kerry's hopeful expression. "'Specially since, as Alex pointed out, there's going to be thousands of entries from camera clubs up and down the country!"

"Well, I don't know about this competition," Meg chipped in, tucking her layered black hair behind her ears as she spoke, "but I'm really impressed that you've managed to stay friends with Alex. I've never stayed on speaking terms with any of my exes!"

"Hey, I've just had a thought..." grinned Sonja. "Can you imagine if Cat didn't speak to her old boyfriends? It would mean she'd never talk to most of the male population of Winstead!"

"Son! Don't be so unkind!" scolded Maya, even though she couldn't stop herself smiling. "Anyway, where is Ms Osgood tonight?"

Sonja rolled her eyes. "Cat's giving The Loud a miss tonight – she's too busy sorting out what she's going to wear tomorrow for her first day of filming with Ben Fitzpatrick!"

"Wow – of course!" gasped Anna. "Matt was telling me about this yesterday. It's so incredible! I still can't work out how she's landed this starring role!"

Kerry and Sonja looked at each other and giggled. "Matt didn't explain it very well, obviously," Sonja grinned, enjoying the chance to put Anna straight about what was *really* going down in her cousin's life. "The fact is, her and Vikki have just been roped in to this production as a couple of extras; you know – walk-on parts in the background. The TV company contacted the college, and they were two of a lucky few available during the holidays."

"Still, that's pretty exciting, even just being an extra!" said Anna positively.

"The trouble is," said Sonja, "Cat's really convinced herself that she's going to get to hang out with Ben Fitzpatrick. In her mind, they're practically engaged! It just hasn't sunk into her head that they keep stars well away from ordinary mortals."

"Does she reckon that getting to know Ben could mean he'll give her a head start with her own acting career or something?" asked Meg.

"Probably!" snorted Sonja. "Though I hate to think what sort of harebrained schemes she's brewing up to make him notice her.

"Oh, don't be so rotten!" Kerry gently chastised her best friend. "I can understand how excited she is – not many girls get the chance to meet the man of their dreams in real life. Every girl in the world goes through a phase of drooling over film stars or singers, and having fantasies about going out with them! It's not so long ago you had that poster of Brad Pitt pinned on the back of your wardrobe door, Sonja Harvey."

"Only *most* girls understand it's just a fantasy," said Sonja, conveniently ignoring Kerry's last point, "whereas Cat believes it can – and will – happen!"

"I guess it's pretty simple really," shrugged Maya. "Cat loves flirting – and, whatever her motives, flirting with a TV star is the *ultimate* flirt!"

"Too right!" grinned Sonja. "Yep – today, Ben Fitzpatrick hasn't a clue who Catrina Osgood is. But, from tomorrow, the poor boy won't know what's hit him! Count on it!"

• • •

"Derek – is it OK if I put one of these notices up?" asked Ollie, holding up a sign that read: *Drummer wanted. Joe is leaving The Loud – in term-time anyway. Can you fill the gap? If you think you can, call Nick or Ollie...*

Derek – the landlord of the Railway Tavern – scanned the A4 sheet, and nodded. "Course you can!" he grunted. "I don't want my Thursday night crowd-puller dying on me for want of a drummer, now do I?"

"Thanks, Derek!" Ollie grinned, his floppy, dark-blond hair still plastered to his forehead after The Loud's energetic set. "I thought about putting a couple up at either end of the bar, and one in the Gents, too."

"Yeah," shrugged Derek, "wherever you want, mate. But how come you're doing it? I thought your manager was supposed to sort out this kind of thing?"

Derek nodded over at his old buddy Nick, who was sitting at a table in front of the stage, along with Cyndi and the rest of the boys in the band.

"Yeah, well, I think Nick's kind of preoccupied at the moment..." said Ollie as tactfully as he could.

Easy-going as Ollie was, he could see that things in the café and the record shop – never mind the band – seemed to be taking second place to Nick's unquestioning adoration for his new wife.

"Can't blame him, though, can you?" chuckled Derek. "Beautiful woman like that..."

"Uh, mm..." said Ollie dubiously, looking over to where Cyndi was giggling and hanging on Nick's every word.

Ollie liked Cyndi well enough, but he was

finding it hard to concentrate at work with her incessant chattering, her insatiable need to change everything in the place and the fact that she stole Nick away from his work at every possible opportunity. It was a bit like having a tornado in the End: lots of noise and activity and, when the dust finally settled, nothing was where it had been before. Ollie still couldn't get over how many flowery, girly things had sprung up in the café overnight. Basically, he was finding it all a bit bemusing – but he knew it was driving Anna mad.

Still, he thought as he left Derek and headed back to the table to get more flyers out of his bag, *as long as all this mushy stuff doesn't go on too long and Nick gets back into action soon, it'll be fine.*

"Hey, Ollie honey!" Cyndi trilled, patting the seat next to her.

Ollie hesitated – he wanted to get the notices up as quickly as possible, before the punters in the pub started to drift away. Still, he could hardly refuse his new aunt...

"I was just sayin' – you guys are amazin'!"

"Thanks!" Ollie smiled, settling himself down on the stool.

"Yeah! And you know what else I was just sayin' to these guys?" beamed Cyndi, indicating Joe and the others.

"No..." Ollie replied warily, sensing somehow that Joe was telepathically trying to let him know what little gem Cyndi was about to impart.

"Well, I really think that the one thing you guys are missin' is an image!" said Cyndi, slapping her palms down on the pub table for emphasis. "You need to get away from them old, skanky army-type pants and T-shirts you wear, and get some style! Somethin' to make you stand out from the crowd!"

"Like?" asked Ollie, raising his eyebrows and feeling a bubble of hysterical laughter rising in his chest.

"Maybe like you could all wear matching shirts!" Cyndi suggested. "Y'know, somethin' smart an' eyecatchin', like a blue and white gingham check!"

"Well, we'll certainly think about it, won't we, boys?" Ollie answered, keeping his face as straight as he could and glancing round at the faces of his friends.

"Oh, hey sorry, lads!" Nick interrupted as he waved over at someone by the bar. "I've got to introduce Cyndi to Derek's missus..."

As soon as Nick and Cyndi had threaded their way through the customers in the busy pub, the five lads exploded.

"Pppffffffffffff!" Ollie spluttered with laughter. "What was she going to suggest next? That we come up with a line-dancing routine and wear matching cowboy hats?"

"She – she said we should all think about getting our hair tidied up too," Billy managed to say, between splutters.

"What's going on?" asked Kerry, scurrying over from the girls' table to see what the band conference had been about.

"Cyndi wants to do a make-over on the band," Matt cackled. "Wants to turn them into cowboys!"

"Well, at least I don't feel so sad about quitting the band and moving to London now," Joe grinned. "I don't think my head is the right shape for a stetson!"

"Hey, that reminds me!" Ollie suddenly said, turning to face Joe. "You know your little problem?"

"Oh, yeah, what's this, Joe? Some secret you don't want to tell us about?" joked Billy. "Is this problem animal, vegetable or medical?"

"Trying to get a flat sorted in London, you idiot," Ollie spelt out to Billy, nudging him in the ribs with his elbow.

"What about it?" asked Joe, curious to know what his best mate was about to say.

"Well, Joey boy," Ollie grinned, "I might just have the perfect solution for you..."

CHAPTER 7

● ●

MUCH ADO ABOUT NOTHING

"...And Lewis said he didn't want to be in my game any more – not if girls were playing too," said Ravi, explaining why he and Kerry's brother had fallen out last time they played in the park together.

"Doesn't he like girls any more?" asked Maya as she and her little brother strolled along the pavement together.

"He says girls are silly," said Ravi matter-of-factly, seemingly unaware that his sister was a girl.

"Does he? Why?" Maya quizzed him, fascinated to know what the average little boy had to say about his female counterparts.

"He says they go all soppy about boys and stuff," he shrugged, scuffing his trainers with every step. "He says that – oh, look, Maya! That's your friend!"

As they approached the junction by the park, it didn't take Maya more than a second to spot Cat hurrying across the road towards them. It was hard not to notice her, as a couple of toots from passing cars proved.

"Hi, Maya!" said Cat breathlessly as her kitten-heeled mules slapped on to the pavement beside them. "Where are you two going?"

"Um, just heading for the dentist – Ravi's due for a check-up," Maya said casually, her eyes flickering over her friend's outfit.

Working up from the turquoise embroidered mules, there was a matching turquoise, silky, knee-length dress with a ruffle at the hem, and a black fringed shawl (also embroidered) tied around Cat's hips. Her bright-blonde, shoulder-length hair had been woven into two short, stubby plaits and around her head she'd tied a trendy denim headscarf, edged in pink velvet.

"Well, I can't stop – I'm on my way to my first day of shooting!" said Cat, her pink-painted lips breaking into an excited smile.

Maya checked out Cat's outfit again. The whole look was great – for a party. But for a TV shoot? Maya was decidedly unsure, but she said nothing.

Was Cat told to dress up like that? she wondered, trying to remember what the drama was meant to be about. Cat had evidently gone to a lot of effort – was it really worth it? *Surely they'll have stuff for her to change into, won't they?*

"I mean, can you believe it?" Cat gushed, clutching her hands to her chest. "I'm *actually* going to meet the *gorgeous* Ben Fitzpatrick!"

"Well, I'm dying to hear all about it – you'll have to get lots of gossip!" smiled Maya, feeling Ravi tugging at her hand. She ignored him. She had a feeling that her kid brother might be about to say something tactless. The way Cat was acting, she was certainly living up to Lewis's theory that girls went all soppy over boys.

"I know we're going to get on really well," Cat continued. "Turquoise is his favourite colour – I read it – so he's got to notice me right away, don't you think?"

"Maya...!" whined Ravi.

"Not now, Ravi, we're talking," said Maya gently but firmly.

"I was just going to say that Ben Fitzpatrick is in Sunny's room," he continued none the less, gazing up at his big sister with his deep brown eyes.

"Huh?" queried Maya, furrowing her finely arched dark eyebrows.

"What do you mean?" demanded Cat.

"She's in love with him!" shrugged Ravi. "She's got posters of him all over her walls!"

This was news to Maya. It was hard avoiding someone who was a member of your own family and living in the same house but, whenever and wherever possible, Maya did just that because she and her sister did not get on. It was as simple as that. One of Sunita's main pleasures in life was to be obnoxious – especially to Maya; for her own sanity, Maya kept as much distance as possible between them. To find that spiteful Sunny had a soft spot for someone or something was quite a revelation.

"Well," said Cat, folding her arms and looking down at Ravi, "just you tell your sister Sunny that *I'm* going to be spending the next week *with* him. In person. *Me*. That should make her good and jealous, shouldn't it!"

Maya winced – she knew Cat was only fooling around, but she didn't really think that her friend's remark was a particulary healthy one for Ravi to hear – or pass on.

"Listen, Cat, we'd better go or we'll be late for the dentist," said Maya, trying to make a swift exit. "And you don't want to be late on your first day of filming..."

"No, I don't!" Cat agreed, wide-eyed. "See you in the End tomorrow morning and I'll tell you all about it!"

"You're on! Good luck!" Maya called as Cat

click-clacked her way along the paving stones.

"Maybe I'll even be able to tell you about our first date!" came floating back over her friend's shoulder.

Maya towed her little brother in the opposite direction. "Close your mouth, Ravi," she sighed. "You know what? I think maybe I understand what Lewis means about *some* girls..."

• • •

Cat blew a large pink balloon of bubblegum and sucked it back in again. She was sitting the wrong way round on a wooden bench by the river, her legs sticking through the gap between the seat back and the seat itself, dangling her pretty mules idly from her toes.

Her chin rested on her hands, her elbows rested on the mossy-green streaked bench-back and her eyes scanned the movement going on at the top of the riverbank, beside the road.

What's taking Vikki so long? She only went for a wee! Cat wondered as she watched for her friend among the small groups of people hanging around by the two location vans.

It had been more than two hours since Cat and Vikki had turned up and presented themselves to Daniel, the TV crew's production assistant. And precisely nothing much had happened since then. They'd met up with Louise, Jason and Darren from Vikki's drama course, as well as some other – older – extras. They'd seen various technical crew wandering around, doing important-looking technical things, and watched as some portable metal fencing had gone up to keep nosy onlookers from getting too close to the action (not that there was any, as far as Cat could see).

And, so far, Ben Fitzpatrick had been absolutely nowhere in sight.

At last, Cat spotted Vikki walking round the side of the larger of the two vans and making her way back down the grassy slope towards her.

"Where have you been?" Cat demanded. "You've been ages!"

"I got talking to Daniel," Vikki explained as she approached.

"Oh, yeah?" said Cat, perking up. "What did he say? When do we get to find out what we're doing? And when's Ben arriving?"

"OK, so do you want the bad news or the good news?" said Vikki, leaning her weight on the back of the bench and looking down into Cat's expectant face.

"Bad news, I s'pose," moaned Cat, lifting one side of her mouth up.

"Ben's not scheduled to shoot anything today,"

shrugged Vikki. "He's at his hotel, doing press interviews."

"You're kidding!" Cat whined. "But that's not *fair*! What's the point in us being here?"

Things were not going at all as Cat had anticipated. She had been certain that she was going to be noticed – that the moment Ben spotted her obvious talent she would be catapulted into stardom, not to mention that he would also, of course, immediately fall head over heels in love with her. But he hadn't even turned up!

Vikki looked slightly irked by Cat's childish response. "What's the point? I'll tell you what the point is, Cat. How about, to get acting experience? To see how filming a TV drama actually works? To make the most of the opportunity?" she suggested irritably.

"Yeah, OK," Cat acknowledged, still sounding down in the dumps at the news of Ben's no-show. "So what are we supposed to do today? And which of the actors are we working with?"

"Erm, that's the *other* bad news – they've decided they don't need us after all today," said Vikki, biting her lip.

"What?!" squeaked Cat, mortally offended. "Why not?"

"Well, Daniel says they're shooting a scene with two of the other actors in it – the ones playing the older detectives – and the only extras they need are a few people feeding the ducks and walking along the path."

"Where's Daniel! Let me talk to him!" said Cat, staring up at the vans in search of the production assistant with his ever-present clipboard. "*I* can feed ducks! *I* can walk along a stupid path!"

"Cat, hold on," said Vikki, trying to pacify her. "They're using that old lady for the duck-feeding and that middle-aged couple for the strolling bit."

Vikki pointed up at the huddle of fellow extras standing together chatting and drinking plastic cups of tea beside the catering table. Cat shot a daggers glance in their direction, giving all three the evil eye for snatching potential roles away from her.

Then she spotted something else that niggled at her – in the small crowd of onlookers hovering the other side of the wire fence, she spotted a face she recognised: Maya's younger sister, Sunny.

"But wait, I haven't told you the good news," Vikki piped up, in an attempt to console her friend.

"Go on then!" sighed Cat.

"Well, Daniel says they *definitely* want us back on Sunday; that's when they're planning to shoot scenes we can be in," explained Vikki.

"And Ben?" asked Cat, brightening up.

"Yes, and Ben should be in those too," Vikki nodded.

"Wheeee!" shrieked Cat, clapping her hands together.

"And the other good news is that Daniel says that since we're down here already, it's fine if we want to hang around and watch today's shooting, as long as we don't get in the way."

Cat frowned up at her friend. "What's the point of that? Nothing's happening!"

Vikki pursed her lips and Cat suddenly realised she was in for another lecture.

"OK! OK! We'll hang about; we might learn stuff; it's for the experience..." Cat trotted out, guessing what Vikki was about to tell her. "Hey, wait a minute – what's going on up there? Why are Jason and Darren getting in front of that camera? I thought you said they were only using the older extras?"

Cat frowned as she watched the two boys from college being positioned.

"They don't need any of us girls – me, you and Louise, I meant."

"And what are Jason and Darren going to *do* in this scene exactly?" Cat demanded.

"Play football in the background apparently," shrugged Vikki.

"Right! That's it!" barked Cat, untangling her legs and getting to her feet. "Where's that Daniel? I'm going to have a word with him – having boys playing football is just plain sexist!"

Vikki rolled her eyes as Cat set off up the slope to go and give Daniel a piece of her mind.

● ● ●

"Daniel, can I have a word please?"

At first glance, Cat felt slightly intimidated by the rest of the film crew – especially the serious-looking director consulting earnestly with one of the cameramen. But there was something about the production assistant that made her feel relaxed enough to talk to him straight. Maybe it was because he looked not that much older than her or Vikki (although she supposed he must be, to hold down such an important job); or maybe it was because he reminded her ever so slightly of two of her closest boy mates.

In fact, that morning, when Daniel had first introduced himself to them and explained *what* was going on and *where* everything was, she'd been struck by how much he reminded her of both Ollie and Joe. Physically – with his floppy fair hair and cute, friendly face, he was like Ollie, while his slightly anxious manner made her think instantly of Joe.

"Sure. What can I do for you, Catrina?" Daniel asked with a smile.

She'd come across him perched on the metal steps of one of the location vans, frantically scribbling notes on the pad clipped to his board.

"Cat, actually," she corrected him.

"Cat – that's a nice name!" he nodded.

She was thrown off balance by his compliment. She'd come to moan about the blatant case of sexism going on under her nose and now he'd taken the wind out of her sails.

"Anyway, Daniel," she said, getting back to the point, "why are Jason and Darren getting to play football in this scene?"

"Um... what do you mean?" he asked, looking a little confused by her question.

"Well, don't you think it's just too predictable? I mean, isn't that just a bit clichéd?" scolded Cat, putting her hands on her hips. "You know, only *boys* play football and *girls* like shopping."

She noticed Daniel's eyes flicker up and down her body. *Is he checking me out?* she wondered. Again, that was a compliment, but cute as Daniel was, he wasn't really her type. Not like Ben Fitzpatrick...

"Well, I see your point – stereotypes and all that – but actually, it's only texture. You know – a bit of noise. Atmosphere. I doubt that they'll feature much in the finished shot," Daniel told her. "Whereas you, Cat..." He paused for a second and flicked quickly through some notes. "Yep, I definitely think we're going to need you a lot from Sunday onwards!"

Cat felt her chest swell at the thought of being so important. That put a whole new slant on things. Jason and Darren were welcome to their little bit of 'texture', kicking a football around...

"Oh and while I think about it—" said Darren, letting his eyes skim over her body again.

He is checking me out! Cat decided to herself.

"—Rhona, who looks after the wardrobe department, asked me to have a word with you about your clothes." Daniel's expression was apologetic. This, Cat realised, meant he wasn't giving her a compliment after all.

"What about them?" she bristled.

"Well, there's nothing wrong with what you've got on – I think it looks brilliant!" Daniel shot her an admiring smile. "But we need you to dress down a bit more on Sunday. You know, wear your ordinary clothes; stuff you'd wear every day."

"But this *is* the sort of stuff I wear every day!" Cat spluttered, even though she knew she had taken hours to choose the exact combination for the right effect.

"And it really suits you. But we need you to wear jeans, or combats and a T-shirt or something,

Cat," Daniel elaborated. "You know – *pretend* you're like an ordinary girl in the street. Rhona might well end up dressing you from the wardrobe, but it's always handy if extras bring their own stuff. It's always more comfortable to be in familiar clothes, don't you think?"

It was on the tip of Cat's tongue to stand her ground; to argue that there was nothing wrong with trying to look pretty, especially in the glamorous world of TV. But two things stopped her – first, she knew she'd only dressed to impress Ben Fitzpatrick (for all the good that had done); and second, she had to remind herself that Daniel *wasn't* one of her mates – he was the guy who was employing her.

"No problem!" she beamed, slapping on her widest Cat smile.

"Brilliant!" Daniel grinned back. "And you know you're welcome to stick around today and watch, if you want to!"

"Definitely!" said Cat enthusiastically. Already her mind was whirring with a new plan.

Dressing in jeans and a T-shirt doesn't mean I have to look boring, she thought to herself. *I think I'll go to Top Shop tomorrow – they've got those new T-shirts in that spell out 'Hi, Gorgeous!' in silver stars on the chest. Ben Fitzpatrick has got to notice me in that!*

CHAPTER 8

• •

THE TRUTH GETS TWISTED

"Wait for *this*...!" Cat treated her friends to her biggest smug smile as they sat round in their regular Saturday lunchtime huddle at the End of the Line.

"What?!" Sonja barked across the table, impatient excitement getting the better of her – and annoyed that her cousin was keeping them all on tenterhooks so successfully.

"There's *only* a wrap party happening next Friday!"

"Wow! That's amazing!" Kerry exclaimed. "Um, what's a wrap party?"

"A party to celebrate the end of filming," Cat informed her friend, as though it was something she'd known all her life.

Actually she'd heard it for the first time the day before. *Over*heard it, to be more accurate.

"And you're invited to the party, even though you're just an extra?" gasped Kerry.

Cat felt her smile falter slightly, but before anyone could spot it, she breezed on. "Yeah, of course I'm invited!" she boasted. "Everyone on set is so friendly! It's like one big happy family!"

If she was Pinocchio, right at that moment Cat's nose would have grown so long it would have been tapping Sonja on the shoulder. The day before, no one apart from Daniel and the guy in charge of catering had spoken to Cat or Vikki – other than a couple of technicians who'd said stuff like, "Could you move out of the way, please?" Cat didn't suppose that really counted.

Darren and Jason had chatted, of course, and Louise, too, who'd hung around to 'observe' filming – the same as Cat and Vikki. But the other, more experienced extras had seemed a bit stand-offish. And the business about the wrap party; well, it was just something Cat had heard two of the actors talking about. She had no idea whether or not it was something she'd get invited to.

Which is why Cat had a new plan buzzing in her head right now; she would have to chum up with Daniel over the next few days and make her lie *become* the truth...

"So where's this party going to be?" asked Maya.

"At the Balinard Hotel," Cat replied casually, "where the crew are staying."

"*Very* nice," nodded Maya, thinking about the beautiful, small stately-home-style hotel just outside Winstead.

"Hold on! Start the story from the beginning!" Sonja put a halt to proceedings, keen to hear *everything* her cousin had experienced the previous day. "Is it really glamorous? Are there hundreds of people on set?"

"Cappuccino for you, Maya," Anna interrupted her girlfriends' conversation as she passed them cups and glasses from her tray. "Kerry, milkshake; Sonja, Coke; Cat, Lilt. That's right, isn't it?"

"Yeah, cool!"

"Thanks, Anna!"

"Thanks!"

"Could I have some more ice in this, Anna sweetie?" said Cat, passing the glass back. Anna rolled her eyes and took the Lilt from her thinking one day on a film set had already gone to Cat's head. Cat, meanwhile, continued holding court.

"Well, it's amazing, but there weren't that many people really. Only about twenty technical staff, the five main actors and a few of us extras."

"How come?" asked Sonja. "How can they do a whole drama with so few people?"

"It's 'cause the bulk of it is being filmed in London," Cat explained knowledgeably, as if she'd been in TV all her life. "The scenes they're doing here in Winstead only need a small crew."

"What's the programme about anyway?" asked Kerry, licking some strawberry foam off her straw.

"It's some police thing, supposed to be based on a true story," Cat shrugged. "It's all centred around Soho in London – a big drugs bust I think – but then some detectives come up and check out leads about some ex-con who's got a new identity in another town, and that's what Winstead is supposed to be."

"Sounds cheery," Sonja joked. "And where does the lusty Ben Fitzpatrick fit into all of this?"

"He's this young detective," Cat sighed.

"So come on then – what's he actually like close up?" asked Kerry, her eyes wide behind her little oval specs.

"Ben?" Cat's eyebrows shot up and she looked momentarily – and uncharacteristically – stuck for words.

"Yeah, *Ben*!" laughed Sonja. "You can't miss him – he's the only celebrity in Winstead that I know of at the present time!"

Cat shot Sonja a withering look. "*Very* funny – I don't think," she muttered. "Anyway, he's – he's fantastic!"

"Is he?" asked Maya, gazing long and hard at Cat. Not that Cat seemed to notice.

"Yes, he's really friendly!" Cat continued enthusiastically. "He came straight over to me and Vikki and introduced himself – he's not a bit starry!"

"And what did he say to you?" Kerry asked in hushed tones, her voice breathless with awe.

"He – he, uh, just said hi," Cat faltered, then remembering her conversation with Daniel, carried on with new inspiration. "And asked our names and stuff – he said my name was nice, and we talked about what I was going to wear when I'm filming tomorrow. Then he got called to go off and do his filming."

"But is he as gorgeous in real life as he is in his pictures?" Kerry asked.

"He's... *more* gorgeous!" Cat announced. "He kept winking and waving the whole time! And he said he was looking forward to working with me a lot from Sunday onwards."

"Well done, Cat – and that's only the first day!" grinned Sonja. "What's it going to be like when you *really* get your claws into him!"

"*Wouldn't* you like to know!" laughed Cat, getting up and squeezing her way out of the window booth, then heading towards the loos.

"Cat and Ben Fitzpatrick!" gasped Kerry, turning to the other girls. "Can you believe it?!"

"No!" said Maya bluntly.

"What do you mean?" asked Sonja, while Kerry looked shocked at their friend's unusually harsh tone.

"Well," Maya found herself smirking, "I happen to know for a fact that Ben Fitzpatrick wasn't even *at* the filming yesterday!"

"How do you know that?" frowned Kerry.

"Sunny – she and her mates found out where the action was and were hanging around at the location virtually all day," Maya explained. "She was telling us about it at teatime last night, and she said Ben Fitzpatrick never showed up. She asked a security bloke there, and he said Ben was spending the whole day doing interviews back at his hotel!"

"Typical Cat!" said Sonja with a sigh. "Why didn't she tell the truth?"

"Just wants to impress us, I guess," suggested Maya. "You know what she's like. She won't want to admit she didn't even get the chance to meet Ben Fitzpatrick, never mind flirt with him!"

● ● ●

"What's going on out there?" asked Ollie, slaving cheerfully over a hot stove.

"Cat's telling the others about her close encounter of the acting kind, I think," smiled Anna, opening the freezer and hauling out a jug full of ice cubes.

"Can't wait to hear that one!" laughed Ollie, holding a spatula in one hand and wiping the hair away from his brow with his other elbow.

"I can!" grinned Anna good-naturedly, dolloping a handful of ice cubes into the tall glass of Lilt.

"Hey, Anna, honey – what's goin' on with that drink?" came Cyndi's voice as she trotted in from the café.

"Uh, well, nothing really," frowned Anna, stiffening slightly as she anticipated some kind of telling off. "Cat asked for more ice, that's all. It's not a problem."

Only the night before, Anna had found herself curled up in her bathrobe, her tarot cards spread out once again on the table in front of her. She'd tried to give herself another reading; to see if it could tell her how to handle the current situation in the café. 'Be patient' seemed to be the answer and, right now, as Cyndi stood in front of her, Anna tried to bear that in mind.

"But, honey, it *is* a problem," said Cyndi, coming over to Anna and placing her arm around her condescendingly. "We've gotta strive to get it right for the customer – first time, *all* the time!"

"But...!" Anna began, trying to explain that asking for more ice, or wanting brown sauce instead of red, or deciding she hated tomatoes in her sandwiches when she'd loved them up till now was just typical Cat – contrary and picky as ever, with no malice intended.

"I'll just take this back out," Anna tried to smile as she slipped out from under Cyndi's arm and headed back into the café.

"She understands, doesn't she?" Cyndi smiled hopefully at Ollie. "She don't take offence?"

"Hey, I guess not!" Ollie tried to laugh, although he wasn't so sure.

"Good!" trilled Cyndi, turning and heading back out into the café herself.

"Did I miss something there?"

Ollie turned round to see Joe hovering tentatively at the back door. "Don't ask!" he grimaced. "So how are you?"

"OK..." shrugged Joe. "But listen, Ollie – about the London thing. I came by to say that I've been thinking and I don't reckon it's such a good idea. I just—"

"Joe!" Ollie interrupted, holding his spatula in the air with a grin. "It's too late! It's all arranged – my plan has worked out and part of your problem is solved! My sister's really cool about you going to stay with her while you flat-hunt!"

Joe's heart sank again – just as it had when Ollie had first told him his idea. Natasha, he suspected, was hardly going to be skipping for joy at the prospect – Joe always got the feeling she considered him to be a bit of a nerd. And as for staying in her flat, with her and her fellow model flatmates – even if it *was* only for a couple of days – the thought left Joe feeling positively sick with nerves...

CHAPTER 9

● ●

FLIRTING – TAKE ONE

"Hi, I'm Dawn, take a seat," said the skinny, friendly-looking woman in the body warmer.

"Hi, I'm Catrina," Cat introduced herself formally as she plonked herself down on the canvas folding seat. "But you can call me Cat!"

She'd been looking forward to chatting to Dawn. For most of this morning, just like on Friday, she and Vikki and Louise had been kept hanging around on the set – this time located by a small shopping arcade in a housing estate on the edge of Winstead. While she'd been waiting for some action, Cat had kept a close eye on the make-up artist. She watched as Dawn had set up her make-up box and brushes outdoors on a trestle table, calling the actors over one by one to get their faces pan-sticked and powdered.

"Well, Cat, what have we got you down for today?" said Dawn brightly as she picked up a clipboard on the trestle table and flicked through it.

"I'm in a scene with Ben Fitzpatrick this afternoon!" Cat informed her, her smile a mile wide.

"Sorry, what did you say your name was? I can't find it on the info sheet Daniel's given me for this afternoon's shoot..." said Dawn, scouring the A4 paper on her clipboard.

"Cat – Catrina Osgood." Cat's heart lurched. Surely the schedule hadn't been changed again? She couldn't bear another day getting nowhere near Ben. But, the truth was, she hadn't seen him around yet – and Cat had been keeping her radar up for any sightings of him for the last three hours.

"And you're playing opposite Ben?" frowned Dawn, her eyes still scanning her info sheet.

"Well," giggled Cat, "I'm not exactly starring *opposite* him. I'm one of the extras!"

"Ah!" exclaimed Dawn, flicking to the next page. "You're one of the three teenage mums who are walking past, pushing prams in the background!"

"Um, yes," nodded Cat, not enjoying hearing how dull that sounded out loud.

When the three girls had arrived that morning and reported in to Daniel, the production assistant had handed them a print-out telling them what their roles were going to be, and what time they should check in with make-up. At that point, Cat hadn't really cared whether she'd be hopping in a frog suit next to him, just as long as she'd be sharing the same space as Ben Fitzpatrick at last. But now, she wished with all her heart that she'd been given more of a chance to shine and be noticed, instead of simply hovering in the background in a scruffy pair of jeans.

Still, for all the dowdy clothes, he wouldn't be able to resist her looks.

Thank goodness for make-up! Cat sighed to herself, glad now that she'd got up so early this morning to get her face and hair just right.

"OK, Cat, so let's get to it!" smiled Dawn, putting down her clipboard.

"Actually, I think I'll only need a little powder," Cat smiled up at her. "You see, I did my own make-up. I'm on a Beauty Therapy course."

Dawn paused and took in Cat's handiwork. Her skin was tanned golden brown, but that hadn't stopped her from adding more colour by way of a browny-pink dusting of blusher on each cheek, with a rich browny-pink lipstick to match. She'd

obviously spent hours doing her eye make-up,
blending a mixture of creams and brown shadows,
and adding a dash of black eyeliner – as well as
lashings of mascara – for a truly film star look. The
hair was film star too, piled up on her head with
artfully teased blonde tendrils hanging down.

"A Beauty Therapy course? Well, good for you!
You look great," nodded Dawn. "The thing is, for
this part, Jon, the director – have you met him?"

"No, not yet," Cat shook her head. "But I know
who he is, of course."

"The thing is," Dawn continued, "Jon's asked for
the extras in this scene to have a natural look."

"A natural look?" said Cat, raising her eyebrows.
"Well, that's what I went for – you know, browny
and pinky shades."

"Erm, it's *more* natural than that," said Dawn, a
hint of apology in her voice as she reached for a
large roll of cotton wool and a bottle of cleanser.
"It's more a case of... well, I'm sorry, Cat, you've
done a brilliant job, but I'm going to have to take
this off and start again."

"Oh!" squeaked Cat, feeling slightly hurt. "Um,
oh, well... never mind. It'll be interesting for me to
see what you do – you know, from a learning point
of view!"

"Good!" Dawn smiled down at Cat. "And I'm

afraid I'll have to take your hair down too. It needs to be pulled back straight into a ponytail. And since it's so obviously bleached, I might brush through a little brown eyeshadow along the parting, so it looks like your roots are growing back in."

As the wet, sticky ball of cotton wool touched her skin and began smearing away all her careful work, Cat froze. She suddenly felt very vulnerable, having her make-up wiped off in the open-air, in full view of everyone. No one – not even her mother – had seen Cat without at least a dash of mascara on for years. And she *always* made sure she spent plenty of time and money hiding her roots – and her real mousey-brown hair colour – from the world.

Now, a whole TV crew was going to see her in the raw. And not just the TV crew: the hangers-on loitering by the nearby barricades – which included, yet again, Cat noticed, Maya's annoying little sister and her mates – would see her like this too.

Her stomach did a flip as the realisation dawned that it wouldn't stop there: Ben Fitzpatrick might arrive any minute and walk past – seeing her with a bare and make-up free face.

Cat felt sick...

"Have you met Ben yet?" asked Dawn cheerfully, like a dentist trying to put her patient at ease. Which is what it felt like to Cat at that precise moment.

"No," said Cat, in a tiny, frightened voice. Somewhere in the back of her mind, she felt – and quickly dismissed – a small pang of conscience about lying so blatantly to her girlfriends the day before in the café.

"He's a gorgeous guy," gushed Dawn, suddenly coming over more like a love-struck girl than the thirtysomething woman she must be. "Great skin. Ever so friendly – that's when you get the chance to talk to him!"

Cat blinked up at the make-up artist, her curiosity beginning to overcome her terror at going 'nude'. And she was glad to see that Dawn had already picked up a tube of foundation. This wasn't so bad – her face would be decent again in no time.

"What do you mean? When you get a chance to talk to him?" she quizzed Dawn.

"Well," said Dawn, speedily smoothing on the creamy foundation with a sponge. "He never has much time to hang out with the crew – he's always whisked away by his publicist the minute his filming is finished. Can you close your eyes for me, Cat?"

Cat did as she was told and felt a soft brush dart here and there around her eyes.

"Yep," Dawn continued. "Apart from Jon the director, the only one who ever gets near Ben for any length of time is Daniel. Actually, I think Daniel probably sees him *more* than Jon!"

"Daniel?" Cat repeated, picturing the stressed but sweet-looking production assistant. She'd seen him only a few minutes before, a frown crinkling his forehead as he sat cross-legged on the grass, hammering at the keys of his laptop computer, bashing out reams and reams of daily updates to print out for everyone later.

"Yeah. Daniel's a real whizz-kid, holding this whole thing together, and he's only in his early twenties. Amazing, isn't it?" Dawn laughed.

Cat nodded, although she didn't know Daniel – or any other production assistants to compare him with – so it was hard to know whether the job he was doing was amazing or not.

"Now can you open your eyes nice and wide?" Dawn instructed her. "I'm just going to put a little mascara on for you..."

Cat was surprised at how amazingly quick this all was. But then Dawn was a very experienced make-up artist. Apart from that, Dawn was only doing the make-up for an extra, Cat realised, and that meant she didn't have to spend as much time on it, since it wouldn't be caught close-up by the cameras.

"Actually, if you're *really* interested," Dawn said

conspiratorially as she flicked away with the mascara wand, "the people worth getting to know on any set are the production assistants. *They're* the ones who know everything and everyone."

I see... mused Cat, staring off at the bustle of cameramen setting up outside the rundown shopping arcade, her eyes trying to search out Daniel, while Dawn gave her face a final dusting of powder. *So I was right – not only might I be able to wangle an invitation to the party out of Daniel, he's probably the best best person to get me an introduction to Ben Fitzpatrick too!*

"There! One natural look – just like that!" announced Dawn, standing back and handing Cat a mirror.

"Wow! You work so fast! I'd love to—" Cat's enthusiasm melted away as soon as she saw her reflection. The foundation made her look pale and washed out; the mascara was so subtle it might as well have been transparent; and the grey-blue 'bags' Dawn had brushed under her eyes made her look like she'd been up all night for a week. It was the perfect image of a stressed-out young mum.

But it certainly wasn't the perfect look for flirting with Ben Fitzpatrick.

• • •

It seemed like they'd been hanging round forever, waiting for Jon the director to give them a signal to start.

"Pretty exciting this acting lark, isn't it? said Louise, sarcastically as she leant on the handle of the pushchair she was in charge of.

"My legs are aching. Can't we sit down for a while? I mean, what could be holding things up for so long?" moaned Cat.

"What about the fact that the star hasn't turned up yet?" Vikki suggested.

"Hey – speak of the devil!" exclaimed Louise. "Look – it's him! It's Ben!"

Sure enough, there was Ben Fitzpatrick himself, walking on to the set with Jon, nodding as he listened to whatever instructions the director was giving him.

Suddenly, Cat found that she was actually glad that her slimline part in the shopping arcade called for her to be pushing a pram. It gave her something to hold on to – the sight of Ben Fitzpatrick in the flesh had made her feel quite faint...

"He's a bit on the small side, isn't he?" Louise hissed.

"He's perfect!" Cat hissed back, her eyes scrutinising every centimetre of his not-very-tall, but undeniably well-proportioned body.

His hair was longer than she'd thought it would be. He'd obviously been growing out the crop he'd had in his last couple of TV shows. But he still had that rough-edged charm, that hint of dark stubble and those amazingly sexy eyebrows.

"They say the camera makes you look pounds heavier," commented Louise. "I'd no idea it made you look six inches taller, too!"

"*I'd* better not stand too close to him – he'll look like an actual-size Action Man next to me!" Vikki chuckled.

"Vik! Don't joke like that!" Cat protested. "He's a star!"

"He's not a 'star'!" laughed Vikki. "He's a working actor, like we all want to be. *And* he's human, don't forget it!"

But Cat didn't hear. All she could think about was that a star – the man of her dreams – was just a few feet away from her. And as soon as the cameras had stopped rolling, she had to find some way to meet him...

Hours later, and an eternity of shoving pushchairs back and forward as take after take took place, the day's shoot was over. Cat's brain flipped into overdrive. Vikki stared open-mouthed after her friend as, without a word, she took off across the set.

"Daniel!" she said, rushing up to the production assistant. "Can I ask you a favour?" Cat might have been talking to Daniel, but her gaze was fixed on Ben, who was once again in earnest consultation with the director.

"What's that?" asked Daniel.

"Can you introduce me to Ben sometime?" she said, coming straight to the point. "It's just that I'm a big fan of his – of his acting, I mean. And I'd love to meet him, but I don't want to go rushing up to him in case he thinks I'm just another autograph hunter or something!"

"Sure," Daniel nodded amiably. "I'll introduce you guys sometime."

"Well, I was thinking... what about now?"

You don't ask, you don't get! Cat told herself, mentally crossing her fingers.

"Um, can't right now," Daniel shrugged apologetically. "He's got to leave in five minutes. There's a car waiting over there..."

Cat glanced over at the sleek, dark Jaguar with its tinted windows. *Five minutes?* she thought. *Well, it's a start...*

"Thanks, Daniel!" Cat chirped sweetly, already hurrying off. "You're brilliant!"

"No problem!" he called after her.

Cat shot off in the direction of her make-up bag,

intent on her second lightning-quick transformation of the day – only this one she hoped would be an improvement. Exactly four minutes later, she emerged – minus the bags under her eyes and plus a dash of pink lipstick and a dash of black eyeliner.

Moments later, she was crouched down beside the flash car, rummaging in her shoulder bag for nothing in particular.

"Lost something, love?" came a voice.

Cat glanced up at the driver of the car, and wondered, from his smirking expression, if he'd sussed her out and knew she was only hanging about in an attempt to see Ben.

"I'm just trying to find my... my purse," she muttered, annoyed that she'd been rumbled.

Feeling herself starting blush, Cat wheeled round and collided heavily with someone who was standing immediately behind her.

"Excuse me..."

Cat glanced up, a shiver rippling her spine. She recognised *that* voice, and it didn't belong to the driver. Sure enough, she found herself clinging awkwardly on to the arm of a very expensive leather jacket. Gazing straight ahead, she found herself almost nose to nose with Ben Fitzpatrick himself!

"Oh, I'm so sorry!" she gasped, hastily letting go of the sleeve – and immediately wishing she hadn't. Ben Fitzpatrick smiled his sultry smile and pulled open the car door.

"That's OK," he shrugged. "No damage done."

For a second, as he slid into the back seat, Ben's sleepy eyes locked with hers and Cat's heart pounded almost painfully.

"Yes!" she whispered to herself as the car purred away. She had met Ben Fitzpatrick. Phase One of her flirting campaign was complete.

CHAPTER 10

• •

(UN)WELCOME VISITOR?

Joe stood outside the door to Tasha's flat – his hand held up ready to knock. But slowly, jerkily, he let it drop.

Should I go back down the main stairs and ring the buzzer at the outside door? he wondered, worried that hopping in through the impressive black door that led into the flats as someone had come out hadn't been such a good idea after all.

He turned on his heels then stopped – rocking back and forth – as he heard music suddenly blast from the flat – a dance track that he recognised as one of Matt's current favourites.

Someone's in! he realised, then shook himself at his stupidity. *Of* course *there's someone in – they're expecting me!*

He faced the door again and had just plucked up the courage to knock once more, when he heard an angry voice yelling above the music.

"*Celine!* Turn that *down*! I'm on the *phone*!!"

Joe fidgeted, hauled his rucksack up on to his shoulder and dropped his other hand down again nervously. *I should go back down...* he decided uncertainly. *Ring the buzzer. Then they'll know I'm here...*

He looked at the stairs, visualising himself hurrying back down them – and got annoyed with himself. This was his chance to get himself sorted – three days in London to get a flat together and he didn't have any time to waste. He took a deep breath and knocked hard, before he had a chance to change his mind or lose his bottle.

"Hello?" smiled a tall, ridiculously pretty girl, looking him up and down once she'd pulled the door open. Her voice, from just that one hello, sounded accented; French, maybe, Joe decided, staring dumbly at her.

He didn't have a clue who she was, and she obviously didn't have a clue who he was either. *Maybe it's the wrong flat!* he panicked. But he knew it couldn't be. Since Ollie had given him the address, Joe had read and re-read it a thousand times.

"I'm... I'm Joe," he managed to splutter out, feeling his face flush red.

The girl pouted her perfectly formed lips and frowned slightly.

"Joe? Ollie's friend?" he tried again.

"Ahh!" the girl suddenly broke into a smile. "You must be Joe!"

"Yeah!" said Joe, relief sweeping over him. "I'm Joe!"

"Come in, Joe!" the girl ushered him in, standing to one side and opening the door wide.

Joe wandered in, tripping over the doormat as he did so. He blushed even brighter red. The girl giggled, making him feel ten times more awkward than he already felt.

"Hold on... no, I said hold on a second... Hey, Joe! Be with you in a second!"

In a blind panic, Joe scanned the huge white and cream decorated room in front of him for the source of the voice. Over on the far wall was a doorway that led through to what must be a kitchen, where a girl with long, long legs and short denim shorts was dancing around to the music while she poured water from a kettle. To his left, a dark-haired girl in a long wispy sundress came out of a room and looked him up and down. The girl who'd let him in was still hovering at his side, looking taller than ever now she was standing right beside him.

But none of those three girls was the source of the voice. A waving hand gave Joe a clue and at last his gaze fell on the girl curled up on the vast cream sofa, dressed in matching cream linen drawstring trousers and a cream long-sleeved top. Natasha had a mobile phone pinned to one ear and was mouthing "one minute" at him.

Joe was about to do something that would make plenty of guys green with envy – spend two nights in a flat with four beautiful models. Only to Joe, being the shy boy that he was, the whole idea seemed like a bit of a nightmare.

Thanks for setting me up with somewhere to stay while I look for a place to live, Ollie, he thought to himself. *But I really wish I hadn't let you talk me into this...*

CHAPTER 11

•••••••••••••••••••••••••••••

FLIRTING – TAKE TWO OR THREE

Cat sat on the grass verge, slowly stewing in the oversized, over-fluffy jumper that Rhona the wardrobe mistress had asked her to put on.

She was due on set at 10.00 am, but it was already 11.45 and she hadn't been asked by anyone to go anywhere or do anything. But after a few days of watching or working on this set, she'd finally come to realise that there was far more sitting around waiting being done than actual acting.

"That's the way it works!" Daniel had shrugged, when he'd stopped long enough to grab a coffee and chat to Vikki, Cat and Louise earlier.

Today, all three girls were having to do more scenes outside the shopping arcade, and Vikki and Louise had disappeared ages ago to get some food while they were waiting. In the meantime, Cat idly watched the technicians drift around busily, testing lighting and taking readings on their sound meters.

While she had nothing else to occupy her, Cat mused on her flirting score with Ben Fitzpatrick over the last few days. It hadn't gone as well as she'd have liked, but now that she'd sussed the potential of using Daniel to get to Ben (he'd promised faithfully he'd introduce them, just as soon as he could) it wasn't exactly bad either.

Sunday had been an excellent start after all, with the physical (if accidental) contact beside the car, followed by that whole eye-locking thing.

On Monday, Ben had been too busy after filming for Daniel to make any introductions, but Cat had quickly sussed out why and used it to her advantage. Ben was being interviewed by a journalist at the side of the set. Cat made sure she and the girls were hovering close by, casually sipping coffee and chatting. Only Cat didn't just chat; she tossed back her blonde hair a lot and laughed out loud, periodically glancing over to check if Ben had noticed her. And there it was again – his eyes locking on hers... and more than once, if she wasn't mistaken.

Today – Tuesday – she'd managed no scores yet on her Flirt-o-meter, but the day was still young.

And, right now, she could see Daniel making his way over towards her...

Brilliant! thought Cat. *I can pump him for information on Ben's movements!*

"Hi, Cat!" smiled Daniel, gripping his ever-present clipboard. "It's all waiting around today again – typical! But don't worry – it's all running to schedule, more or less. Your scene should be set up in about half an hour – OK?"

"OK – no problem," Cat smiled sweetly, though she'd been moaning silently to herself about it not so very long before. "And what about the rest of the week – are we on for any more shooting?"

"Yep, hold on a minute..." muttered Daniel, flicking through copious printed pages. "We won't need you tomorrow, 'cause it's an indoor location with just Ben and the other detective. But Thursday, definitely."

"Where's that going to be?" asked Cat, holding up her hand to shield her eyes from the sun. "Around here again?"

"Um, no... actually, it's at some launderette," said Daniel, reading his notes. "Let's see... it's on Station Road. Do you know it?"

"Do I know it?!" Cat practically squealed. "That's right opposite the café where me and my friends hang out most days!"

"Yeah?" grinned Daniel, his fair eyebrows shooting up at the coincidence. "Well, the old dear who runs the place sounds nice – a location scout set us up with her, but I spoke to her on the phone yesterday just to confirm everything was still all right for us coming."

"Mad Ve— I mean, Vera?" said Cat.

"Vera – yes, that was her name," nodded Daniel.

"Well, that should be fun," Cat replied, hoping the irony wasn't apparent in her voice. She wondered if they'd be prepared for the fact that Vera would probably be harder to keep out of camera shot than all the spectators who'd been hanging around watching the film crew. She'd be waltzing her mop around the launderette before they knew it...

"By the way," she continued, her thoughts returning to her flirting campaign. It was time – now that she had Daniel's attention – to beg another favour. "I meant to ask you, Daniel; somebody was saying something about a wrap party on Friday...?"

"Oh, yeah?" said Daniel. "What about it?"

"Well..." murmured Cat, girlishly tilting her head to one side, "I know I'm *only* an extra, but is there any way I could get invited to the party?"

"Of course! No problem!" Daniel replied, his

face breaking into a friendly smile. "Just come along to the Balinard Hotel around 8 o'clock on Friday and ask for me!"

Cat didn't realise it would be so easy. She decided to push it further... "And can Vikki come too?"

"Vikki? Sure!"

Cat decided to leave it at that. She didn't want to push her luck by trying to wangle invitations for Louise and the boys. Anyway, it was probably just as well they weren't all going. She might get stuck talking to them and, after all, she was on a mission to party with one person in particular...

"Sorry, Cat – I've got to go," Daniel suddenly shrugged. "Stuff to do!"

"You never stop, do you?" Cat smiled up at him, this ball of energy disguised as a boy.

"Nope," Daniel shook his head. "I have to schedule time just to have a coffee!"

As Cat smiled, she noticed Daniel pause and look thoughtful. "Hey, I promised to introduce you to Ben, didn't I?" he said.

Cat nodded.

"Well, I'm off to run through a few changes to the filming schedule with him now," Daniel continued. "Why don't you give us ten minutes, then come over and say hi?"

Cat couldn't stop herself. "Daniel, you're wonderful!"

she shrieked, wrapping her arms around him and giving him a peck on the cheek to say thanks.

Daniel looked a bit stunned.

"Oops!" she giggled, letting go and reminding herself to try to be more professional.

• • •

"You take it white, one sugar, don't you?"

"Um, yeah, thanks," said Daniel, taking the steaming plastic cup that Cat was holding out to him.

"Sorry, I don't know how you take your coffee, so I brought milk, cream, sugar, sweetener – you name it, B—" Cat broke off, suddenly flustered. Now she was actually talking to him, should she call him *Ben*? Not that Mr Fitpatrick sounded right, either...

Cat had taken off the itchy, ugly jumper and wrapped it round her waist, so her 'Hi Gorgeous' T-shirt was in full view. And risking getting in Dawn, the make-up artist's, bad books, she'd also done a quick mascara and lippy fix-up.

"Thanks," Ben Fitzpatrick nodded, taking the other plastic cup Cat was now holding out and shaking his head at the bundle of sachets and cartons on the cardboard tray.

Cat accidentally on purpose let her fingers brush against his.

Those eyes! she sighed to herself. *And those lips! Omigod, he's smiling at me!*

"Yeah, uh, Cat, this is Ben – obviously," said Daniel, finally introducing them. "And Ben, this is Cat – who's doing some extra work this week."

"Cool," said Ben, his voice soft and husky.

"Hi!" giggled Cat, dropping her chin down and peering at her idol through her newly-darkened eyelashes, giving him what she hoped was her sexiest smile.

"How's it going then?" he asked, his eyes fixed like browny-gold laser beams on her face.

Exactly to plan! she felt like saying. "Brilliantly!" Cat gushed. "It's my first acting break – well, on TV, that is. I have acted on the stage before."

"Really?" smiled Ben, raising his famous thick eyebrows.

She was just about to launch into an exaggerated explanation of her two performing experiences, when the laser beams of Ben's eyes turned away from her. It was as if someone had switched off the lights.

"Anyway, Daniel – what were you saying? How many scenes have we got to do before Friday?"

Cat hovered, her girlish smile frozen on her face.

"Um, let me see..." muttered Daniel, flicking through his wedge of clipboard papers. "Tomorrow; that's one... two..."

Cat hovered some more, starting to feel stupid.

"Listen, get me the list typed up and I'll look at it later," said Ben, sounding slightly tetchy. "Now what about those script changes for today?"

"Right here, Ben," Daniel handed the actor yet another wodge of papers detached from his trusty clipboard.

Cat decided it was pointless hovering any more – Ben was talking work and the conversation wasn't likely to swing around in her direction again she could see.

"Well, bye!" she trilled, wiggling her fingers in the air as she backed off.

"Uh, bye!" said Daniel, flashing a fleeting smile.

Ben turned those eyes of his up from the script, setting off a flurry of butterflies in her stomach again. "Good to meet you, Pat!" he called.

"Cat!" she corrected him with a giggle.

"Cat! Of course!" Ben said, and laughed.

So he got my name wrong – so what, she told herself as she walked off to find Vikki and the others. *By Friday night's party, he'll never forget it – or me – again!*

CHAPTER 12

● ●

JOE TASTES THE HIGH LIFE

"Sea Breeze?"

Celine slithered on to the studded leather sofa next to Joe and passed him a tall glass of something pink.

"Um, I guess so," mumbled Joe, taking the glass from her hand. He hadn't known what to order when they'd first arrived at the trendy Covent Garden bar. It didn't seem to sell beer – only an exotic and confusing list of cocktails – so he'd taken the easy way out and just opted to have the same as the girls, even though he hadn't a clue what that might be.

So far, everything about this Tuesday had conspired to confuse and bemuse Joe. After a day of getting lost and exhausted around London (in particular, on the Underground) and *still* not finding anywhere to live, he'd been keen to get back to Tasha's flat in Notting Hill and flop on the sofa – even if the thought of having to chat to Tasha and her three model flatmates filled him with fear. What he *hadn't* expected (and still wasn't sure how it came about) was to find himself steered out of the place twenty minutes later by a gaggle of gorgeous, giggling girls.

And how he'd ended up on a red leather sofa in the sort of bar that was so exclusively hip that you had to be David Beckham or an All Saint to get into defied him altogether. In fact, just as the ferocious-looking doorman turned from Rottweiler to Andrex puppy as Tasha's flatmates strolled in, all Joe could think of was how much Cat would flip when she found out he'd been in one of the celebrity hang-outs that were always being featured in the magazines she so avidly pored over.

Nervously, he watched as the three girls sipped their drinks and thought he'd better do the same.

"Urghh... a-hurgh...!" he choked, as the innocent-looking drink took him by surprise.

"Like it?" grinned Krista, lounging in a leather armchair opposite him.

"It's– it's pretty strong!" Joe managed to say, struggling to get his breath back. "What is it?"

"Vodka, cranberry and grapefruit," said Bee, swirling her ice cubes around with a straw.

"Yeah, it's not usually so potent, but we know Miguel, the barman, so he always puts a little extra vodka in ours," explained Celine.

Joe's eyes were still watering from the shock. It wasn't that he was a stranger to alcohol – he'd helped himself to cold beers out of Matt's fridge in the den often enough. And he wasn't even a stranger to vodka; when he'd had a bad time with depression in the past, he'd taken to drinking the stuff to try and blot out his misery – not that it had worked. But these days he tended to avoid it, not wanting to slip back into his old ways, and the strength of this particular drink had practically set his throat on fire.

Out of sheer nerves, Joe knew he was in danger of knocking back the killer pink cocktail way too fast – and making a huge fool of himself in the process. In a conscious effort to calm his nerves, he carefully placed the glass on the table in front of him, determined to make it last.

"So, Joe – still no luck with the flat-hunting?"

"Um, no, but there's always tomorrow..." he shrugged, feeling hugely shy as three sets of eyes bored into him.

Tasha wasn't with them – she'd been on a shoot

all day and it was running late, as Celine had informed him in the cab to Covent Garden. Not that he missed her company; after all, in all the years he'd been friends with Ollie, he'd never really felt accepted by or comfortable with his mate's twin sister. Even as kids together, she'd always seemed aloof and untouchable, while he'd felt tongue-tied and juvenile in her presence.

So now, here he was, being treated to a night out by three stunningly gorgeous virtual strangers. Celine (French, and the girl who'd answered the door to him) had insisted that he came out with them, even though he'd protested about not crashing their night out, as well as being broke.

"I landed a huge advertising contract today – you've got to help me celebrate!" grinned Krista (South African, and the girl he'd spotted first in the kitchen, wearing the very short shorts).

"Yeah, c'mon! We're not going to take no for an answer!" laughed Bee (Australian, and the girl who'd been wearing the long sundress), scooping her arm under his and frogmarching him out of the door – barely giving him a chance to shower and change first.

Krista brought him out of his reverie. "Yeah, but you're going home tomorrow night, aren't you? That doesn't leave you a lot of time to flat hunt," she pointed out, kicking off her slip-on trainers and folding her long tanned legs into the lotus position on the armchair.

"Well, I've been through all the contacts the university gave me," Joe shrugged, "but I bought this paper Tasha told me about—" He rifled in his rucksack for the yellow newspaper he'd bought earlier.

"*Loot*?" Celine interrupted, reaching out and grabbing the crumpled sheets of paper from him.

"Yes, *Loot*," nodded Joe. "There's quite a lot of choice in there, thank goodness. Tomorrow I'll start ringing round them, and seeing as many as I can."

"But this is going to be too hard!" frowned Celine, her eyes running over the hundreds and hundreds of ads in the 'Accommodation to Let' section. "There are so many flats and in so many areas. How do you know which ones to phone?"

"I don't really," Joe admitted. "I mean, I'd like to stay near university, but it's way too expensive I've found out. I don't really know which other areas to go for..."

And, most of all, what Joe really didn't want to admit was the wave of panic rising in him. Even coming to stay in London hadn't made his search much easier or more successful. He was fast running out of options. And as for selecting from the ads in *Loot*, the only concrete idea he'd had was to close his eyes, wave a pen in the air and phone whatever number it landed on.

The trouble was, when he'd given that a go on the Tube ride back to the flat earlier, his pen had landed on *Lesbian wanted for flatshare in exclusive Hampstead penthouse.* Financially – and sexually – he didn't think he'd qualify for that one...

"Wait a minute!" said Bee suddenly. "I can't believe I didn't think of this before! You know Jake? Jake who works with Frank Lette?" She leaned forward, addressing her words to the two other girls.

"What – Frank the photographer? The one who you did that fashion shoot with last week?" asked Celine.

"Yes, the one with the studio in Shoreditch," Bee nodded excitedly. "But I'm talking about Jake – his assistant."

"Ooh, I remember *him*!" said Krista, her eyes widening. "He's really cute!"

"Cute... and looking for a flatmate!" said Bee, clapping her hands together excitedly and now staring directly at Joe. "I just remembered – he was talking about it during the photo session, asking if I knew anyone who might be interested. But that was before I knew *you* were coming, Joe!"

"But, um, I probably couldn't afford to live wherever he does," Joe squirmed, imagining that anyone working in the media was probably earning a wage that would make his eyes water. At the moment, he couldn't even afford a round of drinks (not at the prices in *this* particular bar, anyway), never mind pay an arm and two legs for some trendy gaff rented by this Jake bloke.

"Joe, do you know how much assistants get paid?" laughed Celine.

Joe turned to face her and shook his head. "A lot?" he suggested.

"A little," she giggled back.

"Peanuts!" said Bee. "So don't worry – he's not looking for someone who's loaded! And the best thing is that he lives five minutes away from the studio. It's all up-and-coming round there in the East End – loads of cool bars and clubs – but it's still pretty cheap at the moment."

Joe's heart thumped slightly, but being the cautious pessimist he was, he wouldn't allow himself to get too excited. "But if it's *that* good, this Jake bloke's probably let it by now," he reasoned.

"Doubt it – his flatmate's not moving out till next month. Hold on…" said Bee, pulling her mobile phone out of her bag. "I'll give Jake a call!"

"Don't worry, Joe!" exclaimed Celine, wrapping a sisterly arm around him. "We'll get you fixed up, no problem!"

"'Course we will!" giggled Krista, leaning over and squeezing his knee.

Out of the corner of his eye, Joe spotted a crowd of young, handsome guys in designer suits at the bar, giving him a look of pure, unadulterated envy...

• • •

"Where are you? It's so noisy! I can hardly hear you!"

Meg might be struggling to make out what Joe was saying, but he could hear her, although he had to ram the receiver up hard against one ear while shoving his finger in the other to do so. He'd refused Bee's offer of lending him her mobile to call his girlfriend, preferring the relative privacy of the payphone instead.

"I'm in some bar in Covent Garden. Zoom-Zoom's or something," he explained, raising his voice.

"You mean Zumba?" asked Meg incredulously.

"Um, I guess so, yes," Joe nodded.

"Wow! That place is so trendy! Loads of famous people go there!"

It was true. In the last hour, Celine had pointed out Kylie Minogue getting very cosy with someone in a booth at the back, while Bee had spotted a whole posse of Australian soap stars. And Joe had actually beaten Krista to it, when they'd both seen a couple of premier league footballers stroll in.

"Yeah, it's pretty hard to get into this place apparently," he said, gazing back along the corridor where the payphone was into the busy bar area.

"So how did *you* manage it!" giggled Meg. "Did Ollie's sister sneak you past the doorman by pretending you were a famous photographer or something?"

"No, she's not even here. I came with her flatmates," Joe explained.

"What — my boyfriend's swanning around London's hot spots with a bunch of gorgeous models he hardly knows?!"

Some girls might have said those same words with quite a different meaning behind them, but Meg spoke with obvious amusement. Joe felt a pang of shame; not so long ago, he'd found himself getting unreasonably jealous if Meg so much as chatted to one of his male friends and now, here she was, being absolutely cool about the situation her boyfriend had found himself in.

At that moment, Joe realised just how much he loved and trusted Meg, and how much she loved and trusted him back.

"You don't have to worry," he assured her, although he could tell by her voice that she didn't need assurance. "I don't think I'm in danger of any of them fancying me. I think they think I'm cute, like a gerbil or something."

"And how's my little gerbil getting on with his flat-hunting?" she teased.

"Good! I mean, it was bad – until about an hour ago!"

"What do you mean?" asked Meg, confused.

"Well, today was bad – everything I went to see had either already gone or was awful," he explained, remembering one overpriced cupboard he'd seen with damp, black mould growing on its walls. Setting up home in the back seat of his Fiat would have been better than that.

"So what happened to make it good?" asked Meg.

"One of Tasha's flatmates knows a guy looking for someone to share with. He's a photographer's assistant, and he sounds OK – I spoke to him on the phone a little while ago. I'm going round to check out his place tomorrow morning!"

"Brilliant!" exclaimed Meg, just as the beeps let them know that Joe's money was running out. "Listen – I'm glad it's working out. And I'm glad you're having fun! I love—"

The line went dead, leaving Joe holding a burring receiver. Meg was right – he was having fun, despite his initial nerves and awkwardness.

Apart from the promise of a flat, there'd been the star-spotting, and the girls' endless funny stories of their modelling exploits. Bee had explained her unusual name to him ("It's Beverley, but my agency are a bunch of snobs and thought Beverley was too naff!"), and they'd got the whole story out of him about being in a band – they'd even forced him to push the sleeves of his T-shirt up so they could coo over his impressive drummer's biceps.

It was funny, Joe realised. If dark and handsome Matt, or Ollie – all cute, scruffy looks and easy patter – had been there at this precise moment, Joe would probably never have got to know these three girls so well. And the same went for Billy with his boundless confidence, as well as Andy, who benefited from the fact that plenty of girls felt comfortable having a gay male friend.

It's like I've been living in their shadow, Joe suddenly realised. *But down here in London – people only know me!*

Joe grinned to himself. He only wished he had a camera on him tonight, so someone could take his photo in this hip place, surrounded by his very attractive new friends. Otherwise, back in Winstead, he might think that the whole thing was some weird and wonderful dream.

● ●

CHAPTER 13

WANTED: DRUMMER. WEIRDOS NEED NOT APPLY

Kerry hesitated for a second, checking her watch and listening for the sound of any music coming from the other side of the door. But there was no music – only the sound of boys' chattering voices.

The auditions must be finished, she thought, feeling confident enough to push the door open, now that she wasn't about to interrupt anything.

"Hi!" she smiled, peering into the large back room of The Swan pub.

"Hey, Kez!" grinned Ollie, his face lighting up. "Fancy trying out to be our new drummer?"

Kerry took in the expressions on the other lads' faces. By the look of it, the auditions hadn't been a roaring success. "Didn't anyone turn up?" she asked, walking across the parquet flooring towards

Ollie, Billy and Andy, who'd set up in the middle of the room, along with Joe's drum kit.

"Yeah – we had four guys show up. None of them were right, though," shrugged Ollie.

"Why not? What was wrong with them?" Kerry quizzed her boyfriend.

"Well, the first one was into heavy metal," Ollie began, "and he played the drums so loudly that he drowned the rest of us out."

"Then the second bloke was just a weirdo," Billy pointed out. "He said nothing; just sort of growled at us and looked well hacked off. I mean he could play OK, but—"

"—we were scared he'd turn into an axe murderer in the dressing room!" laughed Andy, although he didn't look entirely comfortable at the memory of the lad in question.

"Then there was that old guy," Billy recounted. "He could play all right too!"

"Yeah, but he was old enough to be our dad!" Ollie grinned. "I know it's age-ist, but we've got our image to think of. He'd've looked a bit too good in one of those checked shirts of Cyndi's!"

"And that last one... I know *snails* with better rhythm than that bloke!" grimaced Matt, who – as sound engineer for The Loud, unofficial fifth member of the band and delivery man for Joe's drums – had sat in on the auditions.

"So what are you going to do?" asked Kerry.

"We're going to hold Joe hostage and not let him go to London," Ollie told her, completely straight-faced.

"Yeah, we're going to keep him tied up in the dressing room in the Railway Tavern and only let him out to play our Thursday night slot!" Billy joined in.

Kerry rubbed Ollie on the arm – for all the fooling around she knew he must be starting to get worried about what was going to happen with the band. Working for his uncle in the café and the record shop was just his day job to pay the bills. Playing with The Loud was where his heart really lay.

"Anyhow, what are *you* doing here, Kez?" Ollie asked her, trying to sound cheerful. "I thought you were going round to Sonja's after work tonight?"

"Yes, I did," she nodded, "but then Sonja finally decided she should tell her mum and dad about Owen and I didn't fancy sticking around for that."

"What about him?" frowned Matt. "They've been going out for long enough – what's to tell?"

"It's just that she *still* hasn't got round to letting them know she's moving in with Owen when she goes to uni," Kerry explained. "*They* think she's applied for halls of residence and she hasn't got round to setting them straight!"

"Ah..." mumbled Matt, wincing at the notion of the difficult conversation that might be going on as they spoke.

"But aren't her parents really laid-back?" asked Billy, remembering various conversations where Maya and Kerry in particular had been super-envious of Sonja's mum and dad's relaxed attitude; *they* both had to live by fairly strict rules and regulations themselves.

"Yes, but that doesn't mean they're exactly going to whoop for joy when they hear her plans," shrugged Kerry. "I think they wanted her to go into halls and have fun, as well as concentrating on her course. I don't think the idea of her getting all couply and moving straight from home into a flat with her boyfriend is going to please them too much."

"Hey, Kez – could you imagine if we told *your* parents we were moving in together?" Ollie teased her.

"I think my mum would cry for a week and then refuse to speak to me for the next millennium!" said Kerry, rolling her eyes at the very thought. Her mother hadn't even approved of Kerry and Ollie going on holiday together at the beginning of the summer.

"Listen, Kez," said Ollie, sobering up, "we'll be about twenty minutes dismantling all our gear – which'll be pretty boring for you. Why don't you go upstairs to the flat and watch MTV or something?"

"Sure," shrugged Kerry, warming to the idea of lounging around in front of satellite TV, which she didn't have at home. "See you in a bit then. And see you guys later!"

With the boys' goodbyes still ringing in her ears, Kerry pulled at the set of doors that would take her through to the bustling pub. Another quick hello to Ollie's mum and dad (she'd already said hi on her way in), and she could scoot behind the bar and disappear up the internal stairs that led to the flat above the pub.

But as she approached the bar, she hesitated. Ollie's dad was pointing in the direction of the back room, while scooping empty glasses off a table. A girl in a battered leather jacket was nodding, the diamanté stud in her nose twinkling as she did so.

Where do I know her from? Kerry wondered, doing a quick mental flick through the filing cards in her mind.

"Ah, Kerry!" said Stuart Stanton, his eyes settling on her. "Here's someone else who wants to audition for the lads. They haven't packed up yet, have they?"

"Er, no..." mumbled Kerry, feeling slightly

unsettled by the stare she was getting from the all too familiar girl.

"Hi, Kerry," said the girl, with an unsmiling expression on her face. "Remember me? I'm Astrid. I used to fancy your boyfriend."

Kerry's stomach vaulted to somewhere in the region of her lungs. It looked like the growly guy who had come in earlier wasn't the only weirdo they were going to encounter this evening.

Stalker Girl was back...

CHAPTER 14

● ●

INTERVIEW WITH A VAMP

Ollie caught Andy's eye.

"She's good!" Andy mouthed back.

Ollie knew it. He watched as Astrid – dressed in an old Nike T-shirt and faded black army trousers – sat intently hunched over the drum kit, all her energy poured into thundering her way through an old Loud track.

There was no doubt about it: she was head and shoulders above everyone else who'd auditioned that night. And she had the advantage of already knowing a sizeable chunk of the band's songs really well.

All the others who'd turned up had just hammered out a few drum solos, while the boys tried to join in on their guitars; whereas Astrid had immediately suggested playing along with a couple of their songs.

Ollie flicked his gaze at Billy to see what he thought. Billy gave him a quick nod, his eyebrows shooting up in surprise. He was impressed too.

"That was... um... great, Astrid," Ollie acknowledged as the last bars of the song ended. As he spoke, Ollie could feel there was something strange about his face – plain, old-fashioned shock had contorted his muscles so he looked like a spooked caricature of himself. Still, that was only to be expected. After all, it wasn't *every* day that your ex-stalker auditions to join your band.

"I know," said Astrid, straight-faced.

She got up from behind the drum kit and pulled on her oversized leather jacket.

"Well, we've got a few people still to see, so I guess we'll let you know..." Ollie said, trying to sound professional.

None of the other lads had said anything since the moment Astrid had walked through the door with Kerry and asked to try out for them. Kerry too – sitting at the side of the room instead of watching MTV as she'd planned – was saying nothing.

"Look," Astrid announced suddenly, running a bony white hand through her short spikes of black hair. "I know you all think I'm a nutter—"

She paused momentarily, but no one was about to jump in and contradict her.

"—but I'm not. I've changed. I don't trail bands any more. I don't get hung up on lead singers. I'm over all that obsession stuff."

Ollie gulped. There was something unsettling about looking at the girl's intense face and hearing her state something so frankly like that.

Astrid wasn't a particularly pleasant memory for Ollie: she had turned from an enthusiastic fan of The Loud to crazed obsessive, acting like she expected to be Ollie's next girlfriend – even though a) Ollie was already going out with Kerry and b) he'd never given her the slightest encouragement. And the way Astrid had followed him around, giving him little presents and messages had gone beyond a joke – it got quite spooky. The nickname Stalker Girl had suited her very well indeed.

The situation had been further complicated when they found out that Astrid's dad was Derek, who ran the Railway Tavern. Ollie had found it hard to tell the bloke who hired the band that his daughter was seriously freaking him out.

Luckily, Astrid had got bored with the band (and Ollie) as quickly as she'd become obsessed. The lads had heard and seen nothing more of her – assuming she'd moved on to another unsuspecting group.

"I've got this new mate at college," Astrid continued. "She's studying psychology."

Ollie gulped again. Where was this going? With Astrid, it was hard to tell.

"I've spoken to her about a lot of stuff in my life. And she told me I was confusing attraction for people in bands with my love of music," Astrid announced matter-of-factly. "She told me I should try learning to play an instrument – get into music myself. So I took up the drums and I love it – and it's a great way of getting rid of my pent-up aggression, y'know?" she added, fixing Ollie with a dark-eyed stare that cut through him like a laser beam.

Ollie gulped, then nodded and managed a smile. Maybe Astrid *had* changed, and maybe he'd never have to worry about her trailing him and leaving him presents again, but this odd girl still managed to freak him out.

"So there you go," shrugged Astrid, having laid all her cards on the table. "Call me to tell me one way or the other, yeah?" She held out a torn piece of paper which Ollie took tentatively, then she walked to the door.

Turning back before leaving, she treated them all to another penetrating stare. "I'd be good..." And then she was gone.

Ollie sighed silently to himself when he saw there was only a mobile phone number scrawled there. He'd half-expected to see a bleeding heart with both their names doodled on it...

• • •

"I forgot to ask her – how did she even find out about the audition?" blinked Billy, suddenly finding his voice again now that Astrid had gone.

"Duh! Her dad's pub remember?" Andy pointed out. "Ollie put posters up in there."

"God, yeah of course – I forgot about that!" said Billy.

"Yeah, well, just 'cause she doesn't come to watch us any more," shrugged Ollie, "it doesn't mean she never goes in her own dad's pub!"

The four boys – plus Kerry – sat in thoughtful silence for a moment around one of the picnic-style tables outside The Swan. Despite a light evening wind that was threatening to blow away their open crisp packets, it was still warm and the passing traffic had slowed to a trickle.

"You've got a real problem there, though," Matt chipped in eventually.

"A problem – how?" asked Ollie.

"Well, Astrid was *miles* better than any of the

others that showed up tonight," Matt stated.

"He's right," mumbled Andy, spinning his empty glass around in front of him. "She might not've been playing all that long, but she's a natural."

"And I guess it *would* look pretty cool – having a girl drummer and everything," said Billy, almost apologetically. "I know you were joking about our image, Ol, but think about it, mate..."

Matt, Andy and Billy looked at Ollie and waited to hear his verdict. Obviously, *he* had been the one who had suffered the most from Astrid and her strange ways in the past – so it was up to him to decide which way to go with this.

"I think..." he began, as the others hung on his words. He reached over the table and took his girlfriend's hand in his. "I think me and Kerry need to have a chat about this first..."

CHAPTER 15

● ●

AN UNEXPECTED CONVERSATION

Joe could hear the flicking of paper coming from the passenger seat, where Natasha sat skimming her way through the copy of *Elle* in her lap.

It was Wednesday afternoon and Joe was on his way back to Winstead, after *finally* landing himself a flat. He'd found his way to the East End that morning (which was a minor miracle after one too many Sea Breezes the night before) and met Jake. He'd checked out the flat, hit it off with Jake, and said yes – with great relief – to moving in.

"I take the next on the left, don't I?" he asked, breaking the silence.

"Yeah, that's right," Tasha replied, glancing up from the fashion pages she'd been studying and checking the upcoming road signs. "And thanks for driving me, Joe – this location is a nightmare to get to; I had to take three trains and *still* ended up in a taxi yesterday!"

They were on the outskirts of London now; Joe was taking a slight detour from his route home so he could drop Ollie's sister off at a shoot. She'd asked him that morning and, after putting him up for a few nights, it was the least he could do.

"So you're coming to live with us then?" said Tasha suddenly.

There'd been just one problem with Joe's new flat – the overlap between the start of Joe's course and Jake's present flatmate moving out. But it wasn't really a problem; Bee and the other girls had already told Joe that their sofa was his till he could move in to Jake's.

"Uh, well, just for a week or so," Joe said nervously, his eyes on the motorway ahead of him, scanning for the upcoming turning he was meant to take. "I mean, if that's OK with *you*."

Joe wasn't sure if she was annoyed or not – since he'd arranged all this with her flatmates, not with Natasha herself: firstly, because Tasha had hardly been around to speak to in the last few days anyway, and secondly, because Celine, Krista and Bee had insisted.

"'Course I don't mind you staying with us!"

shrugged Tasha. "It's no problem. Celine and the others seem to really like you – and we're hardly ever all at the flat at the same time anyway, so there's plenty of room."

Joe felt the colour flood to his cheeks and hoped that Tasha wouldn't notice. He wasn't used to compliments, especially from pretty girls. His mind suddenly shot back to early that morning, when he'd been woken by a kiss; Krista had landed a smacker on his forehead to say goodbye before she hurried off to a photo-shoot. And Bee and Celine had been just as sweet, fussing over him at breakfast before they too had to disappear off to castings and appointments of their own.

Only Tasha had hung around, asking Joe if she could scrounge a lift from him.

"So, come on – you've hardly told me anything about her! Give me the gossip on my brand new Aunt Cyndi!" Tasha suddenly announced, slapping her magazine shut.

"Well, like I said," Joe shrugged, heading down a sliproad, "she's, er... nice enough."

"Oh, Joe – I'm sure you can do better than that!" probed Tasha. "My mum's already told me that Cyndi looks like Dolly Parton's younger sister. And my dad thinks Nick's lost his marbles!"

"What about Ollie?" asked Joe. To him, it

sounded as if Tasha might already have a pretty good idea of what was going on at the café, but he reckoned he might as well err on the safe side before he opened his mouth and put his foot in it.

"Ollie just says it's gone a bit peculiar. He says Cyndi is putting lace and doilies and flowers everywhere, and Nick's so doe-eyed he's letting her do exactly what she wants."

"That's about the size of it," Joe shrugged. "You won't recognise the place when you come home next time!"

"I bet all those fluffy feminine touches are going down a bomb with the granny brigade!" Tasha joked.

"Yep!" Joe grinned. "They love it – and the corny country music that's on the jukebox now!"

"I'm dying to see the expressions on the other customers' faces! What about all the workmen that come in? And everyone from school?" Tasha pointed out. "The End isn't exactly going to be a cool hang-out now!"

"Tell me about it! There's this bunch of bikers that turn up now and then and, the other day, they parked outside the End, walked up to the door, took one look at the lacy curtains in the window – and got straight back on their motorbikes!"

Natasha began to giggle and Joe couldn't help

joining in. But for Joe, it wasn't just to do with the remark he'd just made: it was also to do with relief. He'd been dreading the thought of being stuck in Tasha's company for the hour he'd reckoned it would take to drive to the location. He'd had so little to do with her over the years, and had so little in common with her, that he'd imagined aching silences between them that only the car radio could fill.

Instead, they were chatting easily and even having a laugh into the bargain. Who would have thought it...?

"Oh, look, we're here already! That's the hotel we're shooting at!" Natasha pointed out as they passed a clump of trees and an ornate Victorian building came into view.

Joe indicated, turned into the long, gravelled drive and drove slowly up it.

"By the way, I don't mean to be bitchy about my Uncle Nick getting married – I'm really happy for him," Tasha said. "Good luck to them. I can't believe it, but I'm a bit jealous!"

"Jealous?" frowned Joe.

"Yeah, jealous of people being madly in love. I wouldn't mind some of that for a change!"

Joe didn't reply – he was too busy dealing with a sudden pang of longing for Meg. He couldn't wait to see her later tonight; he was planning to drive to her house just as soon as he'd dropped off his bag at home and had a chance to fill his mum in on what was going on.

"Of course, *you're* one of the lucky people, aren't you, Joe?" smiled Natasha. "You've been going out with what's-er-name – Meg? – for ages now..."

"Yeah, but I don't know why," Joe tried to say casually, although he could feel that a happy/shy/stupid look had come over his face at the mention of his relationship.

"What are you on about?"

"It's just... well... Meg is just really something," he shrugged, struggling to find the right words. "And sometimes... sometimes I just can't figure out why someone like *her* wants to go out with someone like *me*."

"What do you mean, 'someone like you'?" asked Natasha.

Joe pulled the handbrake on as they arrived outside the hotel's main entrance and said nothing. He found it hard to put his own insecurity into words. Even if Meg had made him feel a hundred times more secure about life, he still found it hard not to think of his negative points when it came to talking about himself.

Sensing his embarrassment, Natasha steamed right in. "Can I tell you something, Joe?" she said as she shoved her magazine in her bag.

Joe shrugged again.

"I always thought you were one of the sweetest boys at school," she smiled. "Most of the other guys were real idiots – really rude and loud and obnoxious. But you – well, I knew you were shy and everything – but you seemed so gentle and nice. No wonder Meg loves you!"

And with that, Tasha pecked him on the cheek, swung herself out of the car and was gone with a cheery wave.

Joe waved back, stunned at this revelation. In the last twenty-four hours he'd been fussed over and had more compliments from beautiful females than he knew what to do with...

CHAPTER 16

● ●

PAT'S BIG BREAK

"Lordy – what is that ol' lady doin' exactly?" asked Cyndi, stopping as she passed by the window booth to peer out of the lace-edged pane of glass at the scene unfolding on the other side of the street.

Anna, on her way back to the kitchen – where Ollie was busy tidying after the lunchtime rush – stopped and stared over at the huddle of people and vans outside the launderette. When she caught sight of Mad Vera, she smiled. She had a real soft spot for the old dear.

"Whatever it is, I don't think that bloke knows how to handle it!" she grinned, watching Vera holding up her skirt a little and doing something that was vaguely like tapdancing, while an embarrassed guy in a baseball cap watched.

"That's Jon," Vikki explained. "He's the director. Not that we've ever been introduced or anything. Us extras are too lowly for that!"

Before Cyndi and Anna had joined them, Vikki, Maya, Sonja and Andy had been lounging in the window booth, enjoying their ringside seat to the filming opposite. Vikki's stint as an extra was over, while Cat was to be recycled as another background character, with the help of the make-up and wardrobe crew.

Not that they'd caught sight of their friend yet. Or the star of the show himself.

"Who's that talking to Vera now?" asked Anna as a young, good-looking lad with a clipboard gently manoeuvred her away from the director.

"That's Daniel – the production assistant," said Vikki. "He's the person we know best on the set. He's cool."

"Mmm, cute too!" said Sonja appreciatively.

"So what's happening with this actor bloke?" Maya asked with a smile. "Hasn't Cat managed to make *him* the person she knows best yet?"

"Not for the want of trying!" grinned Vikki. "She's been flirting her little heart out, but I don't know if it's got her very far! "

"But you're both going to the wrap party tomorrow night, aren't you?" Maya pointed out.

"Maybe that's when all Cat's efforts will pay off!"

"Yeah – that's what she's hoping for," nodded Vikki.

"Wow, I wish I was going. I'd love to go to a party with glamorous TV people!" Sonja sighed.

"Me too – even though no one, even that cute production assistant lad, looks very glamorous from here," joked Maya. "So Vik, you can't do a bit of flirting yourself and wangle us in, can you?"

Vikki shook her head. "Only cast and crew, I'm afraid!" she shrugged. "I think we're the only extras going – thanks to Cat! She hasn't been restricting her flirting to Ben Fitzpatrick, you know – Daniel's been getting her attention pretty full-on too."

"Hey, look – is that Ben Fitzpatrick there? Getting out of that car?" asked Andy, squinting out of the window.

"Yep," nodded Vikki. "That's him!"

"Bit small, isn't he?" Sonja remarked.

"A lot of famous people are small, though, aren't they?" mused Maya, her eyes locked on the antics going on across the road. "I mean, Tom Cruise is supposed to be quite short, isn't he?"

"It's all to do with proportions," Vikki told them. "You can never tell how tall or short anyone really is just by seeing them on screen."

"Check out all those fans goin' crazy!" laughed

Cyndi, leaning her taloned hands on the table.

It was true. As soon as Ben Fitzpatrick got out of the car and made his way to the set, a gaggle of girls went mad – calling out to him from behind the metal barriers and holding out their arms towards him.

A security guard was standing close by them, making sure that no one got too overexcited or tried to make a vault for it.

"Aw, look," Cyndi continued. "One of 'em's got a bunch of roses – an' she's tryin' to get his attention!"

They all focused on the girl, who looked like she was about to topple over the barrier, she was leaning so far over. Not that Ben Fitzpatrick was taking any notice.

"Maya," Anna began, "isn't that—"

"Sunny? Yes, it certainly is..." Maya sighed, staring at the unfamiliar distraught and desperate expression on her sister's face.

For once, Maya almost felt sorry for her.

• • •

Cat slid a finger gingerly under her wig and tried to reach the itch without dislodging it. She'd never realised how scratchy and annoying these things could be and, with the summer sun blazing down, her head was overheating uncomfortably too.

Just as her nail finally hit the spot, she froze – there in front of her was Ben Fitzpatrick, flopping down on the make-up chair. For a second he looked straight through her, then sudden recognition sparked that trademark, warm smile of his.

"Hey, Pat!" he called out to her.

"Cat!" she corrected him.

"Right! Sorry, Cat," he repeated, slapping himself on the forehead. "Anyway, Cat – have you seen Dawn? She's supposed to be here."

"She's just gone for a break, I think," Cat replied, practically breathless with excitement at this chance encounter – *really* by chance, this time. "I don't think she was expecting you so soon..."

Ben frowned, his dark eyebrows knitting in irritation.

He even looks gorgeous like that, Cat thought.

"What a bore!" Ben sighed. "I only need powdering down. I want to get back on set asap – there's a tricky bit I need to go through again before we shoot."

Cat gasped, then held her breath. Was fate was smiling down on her? It was like Cinderella all over again when Cat – who'd helped the lead actress learn her lines – had taken her place in the college panto when the actress got sick. Only this was *far* more exciting than any college panto. Here was one of Britain's hottest young actors, with no make-up artist around to help him out. And what was Cat training to be (until she got her own big break in showbiz)? A make-up artist – to stars just like Ben.

"Well, I can do that!"

The words were out of her mouth before she'd even realised she was going to say them. Almost gulping at her own daring, Cat put out a slightly shaking hand to the powder puff she'd seen Dawn using so often over the last few days. Hastily draping a protective gown round Ben's shoulders, she deftly patted the pad over Ben's chiselled (and, as far as she could see, completely non-shiny) features. Then, completely unable to stop herself, Cat gently smoothed her fingertips over Ben's eyebrows and around the edges of his lips.

Ben opened one eye. "Problem?"

"No, not at all. Just getting rid of the excess..." Cat hastily invented. Sliding one hand either side of his head, she untucked the gown from around his neck – suddenly even more aware of just how deliciously close she was to the man of her dreams. "All finished," she sighed regretfully.

Ben stood up at once and took a quick peek in the mirror. "Thanks, Pat. You're a darling. See you later."

Leaning towards Cat, Ben brushed his lips against her cheek – and then was gone. Cat stood transfixed to the spot, barely able to believe what had just happened. Ben Fitpatrick had *kissed* her. *Kissed* her! Forget that he'd called her Pat again. "See you later," he'd said. Her flirting plan was finally paying off.

Who says celebs aren't interested in ordinary people, Maya Joshi? Cat mused gleefully, replaying the last few seconds over and over in her head. Had he really had to stretch up to reach her cheek? Surely not. He was just trying to get closer, without being too obvious. *Maybe he'll change his mind about the run-through and come back. Or, maybe he'll decide he wants me to help him on set, too. Any minute, I might hear the sound of footsteps behind me, and then I'll hear—*

"Cat!"

The sound of her name broke Cat's reverie, and she whirled round, heart thumping wildly. "Yes, Ben?"

But instead of locking eyes with the lovely Ben Fitzpatrick, Cat found herself face to face with Daniel, his features taut with stress, his knuckles white with tension where they clutched the edges of his ever-present clipboard.

"Cat, you know you said that you and your

friends hang out at that little café across the road?" he bleated.

"Yes," she replied, trying to hide her disappointment.

"Well, are any of them in there today? It's just that Jon wants some older teenagers in the shot and I thought maybe – if they were up for it – they could help out?"

"Yeah, I could go and see who's there, I suppose," Cat shrugged half-heartedly.

"Great!" Daniel smiled with relief. "Those girls that have been hanging about are too young and I don't want to hold up the schedule by having to cast some new extras."

"OK – I'll go over to the End and see who I can round up," Cat told Daniel flatly.

"Just anyone in their late teens – and normal!" Daniel called after her as she walked off. "They've just got to hang about outside the launderette and chat!"

"Whatever," muttered Cat, feeling a little down after her earlier elation. For once in her life, the last thing she felt like right now was being watched by all her friends...

● ● ●

"Hey, Vikki – come here quick!" called Sonja urgently as Vikki made her way back from the loos.

"Yeah – some woman from the shoot is crossing the road and it looks like she's coming here!" Andy joined in.

"What does she look like?" asked Vikki, hurrying back to the window seat.

"In her thirties, mousy-brown bob, bit housewifey..." Sonja called out as Vikki slid back into the banquette.

"I don't know..." frowned Vikki, failing to recognise the description. "Must be a new extra..."

"That's no new extra!" said Maya as the housewifey women suddenly gave the girls a wave. "That's Cat!"

"What? Where?" asked Andy, leaning forward for a better look.

"My God!" gasped Sonja, only now recognising her cousin as she walked up to the café door.

"When are the next Oscars?" Andy suddenly quipped.

"Why?" asked Vikki.

"'Cause the make-up and wardrobe people on this programme deserve an award for transforming Cat into *that*...!" he grinned broadly.

"Daniel, this is my cousin Sonja," said Cat, doing the introductions, "and these are my friends Maya, Andy and Ollie."

"Hi!" A much more relaxed Daniel grinned at everyone in turn. "Thanks for helping out! If you four could just stand around here—" he pointed to a spot on the pavement in between the launderette and the newsagent next door "—for the next shot. Just chat among yourselves, pretend we're not here. It's just a very quick exterior shoot – all the main scenes are set inside the launderette, so it shouldn't take too long."

"No problem! Take your time!" laughed Ollie. "I'm supposed to be working, so I'm in no hurry to get back!"

"So, Daniel, do we need to get anything done to us?" asked Andy shyly, running a hand through his black hair. "I mean, do we need to get make-up on or get changed into other clothes or something?"

"Nah," Daniel replied, giving them all a quick once-over. "We won't see you close up. And the clothes you're wearing are fine. Well, maybe not *that*!"

Strangely, Daniel seemed to be pointing at Ollie's groin. Ollie looked down – as everyone else was doing – and burst out laughing. "Didn't you know? Pinnies are in!" he quipped, tugging off his work apron and scrunching it into a ball.

"Here, give me that," said Cat, holding her hand out. "I'll give it to Rhona in the wardrobe department – you can get it back from her when you finish."

"Uh, OK, guys, looks like I'm wanted elsewhere," Daniel announced, staring over at a technician who was trying to get his attention. "I'll be back before we shoot. Just relax, OK?"

"Very cute!" Maya muttered to Cat as they watched Daniel hurry off.

"Definitely!" agreed Andy.

"Ah now, Maya saw him first!" joked Sonja, wagging a finger at Andy, who grinned but didn't take his eyes off Daniel's retreating figure.

"Yeah, I guess he *is* cute," Cat shrugged, "but he's nowhere near as gorgeous as Ben Fitzpatrick!"

"How's it going with him anyway, Cat?" asked Ollie, sneaking a peek inside the launderette, where Ben was being positioned by the director, under a bank of bright spotlights.

"You'll never guess—" Cat began, then stopped herself. *No, I'm keeping this to myself, for the moment,* she decided. She scratched under her hot wig again, dislodging it slightly. "I'm taking the subtle flirting approach with him at the moment," she improvised.

"Subtle? You?" snorted Sonja.

Her cousin gave her a withering look. "Yes, subtle," Cat repeated. "Just hanging around, giving him meaningful looks, talking to him when I can... that sort of stuff. We've got a connection, you know. And, of course, tomorrow night's the wrap party..."

"Cat, if you're looking for another excuse to talk to him, you could do me a favour at the same time," said Maya suddenly.

"Huh?" frowned Cat, narrowing her eyes.

"Well, could you ask him for an autograph?" Maya explained, pulling a pen and a piece of paper out of the small drawstring bag she had slung over her back.

"Sure!" Cat nodded. "I'll ask him later." She was more than happy to have another excuse to get close to Ben, even if it didn't seem like Maya's style to ask for an autograph.

"Cat – can you get into position, please?" Daniel called suddenly from inside the launderette.

As she shot off, Sonja called after her. "Hey, Cat!"

"What?" said Cat, pausing in the doorway.

"Now that we're actors," grinned Sonja, "does

that mean we get an invitation to this fancy party tomorrow night?"

"No!" Cat replied archly.

"Hey, Cat!" Sonja called out again, making her stop in her tracks once more.

"What now!" grumbled Cat.

"Your wig's gone wonky!"

To the sound of her friends' laughter, Cat sighed, straightened her wig and disappeared.

CHAPTER 17

● ●

ANNA MISSES OUT

"...it was so spooky – it's just that *that* is what Cat could look like in fifteen years time, if she let her hair go back to its natural colour!" exclaimed Sonja as everyone crowded round the pub table.

There was still half an hour to go before The Loud took to the stage and the lads were in no hurry to go to their dressing room. For once, swapping tales about the events of the day was far more interesting.

"Yeah, but what are the chances of Cat ever giving up her addiction to bleach?" joked Matt, sitting with his arm around Anna. Like Kerry, Billy, Joe and Meg, he'd missed out on the chance to be in Ben Fitzpatrick's TV drama, but he was enjoying hearing about it anyway.

"But are we actually going to see any of you on the telly?" asked Billy. "I mean, how close was the camera?"

"Well, we had our backs to it," Andy grinned. "All except you-know-who – who got his mug right in there!"

"I couldn't help it!" Ollie protested. "That guy Daniel just told me to stand there like that!"

"You should have been wearing a T-shirt with 'The Loud' written on it," commented Andy. "The band could've got a free plug on TV!"

"Hey, maybe we could offer to do the theme music for the programme!" Ollie suggested enthusiastically.

"Yeah, talk to Cat about it when she turns up," said Billy, getting carried away with the idea. "She could give that Ben a tape of ours!"

"She'd love that!" laughed Sonja. "It'd be yet *another* excuse to talk to him!"

"Yes – when I asked her if she could get Ben's autograph for Sunny, she was more than happy to help out," Maya grinned.

"Is your sister a fan of Ben's?" Meg asked Maya.

"*Is* she? She nearly cried when I gave her the autograph!" smiled Maya, still reeling from the genuine thanks she'd got from Sunny when she'd handed over that little surprise earlier in the evening. Having Sunny show gratitude towards her was even *more* shocking than seeing Cat in a dowdy wig.

"Right – I'm going to the bar," announced Matt, getting to his feet. "Who wants what?"

"I'll give you a hand," said Anna.

"What's up? You've been a bit quiet..." Matt remarked as he and Anna squeezed through the crowd hanging around the counter.

"Oh, I'm all right," Anna smiled. "I'm just feeling a bit sorry for myself and it's stupid really..."

"Hey, come on!" said Matt with concern, wrapping his arm around her waist. "What's up? You can tell me anything – even if it *is* stupid!"

"Well... I ended up feeling a bit like Cinderella today," shrugged Anna.

"How come?" asked Matt.

Anna scrunched her nose up as if what she was about to say was embarrassingly silly. "It's just that when Cat came into the café and asked if any of us could come and be in the filming," she began, "Cyndi was all for Ollie going over with Andy and the girls. It was like, 'Go on, Ollie! Go an' have fun with the other kids. Me and Anna'll manage here!'"

Matt could see why his girlfriend felt upset.

"Whether she means it or not, Cyndi makes me feel like a second-class citizen!" Anna sighed, wrinkling her nose again and looking downhearted. "D'you know what? I don't even have a set of keys for the café any more. Cyndi 'borrowed' mine the other day – and she's never given them back."

"C,mere, Cinders, Prince Charming wants to kiss you," he grinned, pulling her close.

Anna had just wrapped her arms around Matt's neck, when an insistent coughing began behind them. She ignored it, but it started again – louder. Breaking apart from their kiss, they turned to see who was trying to attract their attention.

Cat gave them a 'caught-you!' smirk. "Sorry to butt in – but that was looking like an X-rated snog and this pub is only PG-rated, I'm afraid!" she teased.

"Thanks – nice timing!" groaned Matt.

It was then that Anna noticed the boy standing by Cat's side. She recognised him vaguely, but couldn't quite place him. Or maybe she just *thought* she recognised him because he looked a little bit like Ollie, with his friendly grin and scruffy fairish hair.

"Anyway, if you two can keep your hands off each other long enough to be polite, I want to introduce you to Daniel here," Cat replied.

Ah, the lad with the clipboard! Anna thought to herself, now placing the face.

"Daniel's the production assistant on the shoot," Cat explained for Matt's benefit. "And Daniel, these are my friends, Anna and Matt."

"Pleased to meet you," Daniel smiled, his hands – without a clipboard to clutch – shoved deep into his trouser pockets.

"Same here," nodded Matt. "So Cat managed to persuade you to come and check out the band tonight, did she?"

"I suddenly thought of it, when I realised it was Thursday," Cat jumped in. "But Daniel was the only one who was up for it!"

Anna felt Matt squeeze her hand – he was obviously thinking the same thing as her: Cat had issued a general invitation in the hope that the lovely Ben might take it into his head to turn up too. But that didn't seem to have happened.

"Yeah, it's good to take an evening off for a change," nodded Daniel, glancing around the pub and letting his eyes settle on the stage. "And I got talking to one of the guys in the band after shooting today. He invited me too."

"Who? Ollie?" frowned Cat. It was the first she'd heard of it – she thought Ollie had scurried back to the café as soon as their scene was over.

"No – the lad with the black hair." explained Daniel.

"Oh, Andy," shrugged Cat. "Well, anyway, come over and meet some of my other friends..."

With an apologetic look over his shoulder at Matt and Anna, Daniel found himself steered away, towards the table where Joe, Billy and the others were sitting.

"She's loving this, isn't she?" Matt whispered. "Showing off the fact that she's swanning around town with someone from a TV crew!"

Anna smiled. "Yeah, but I think she'd rather be *snogging* the star!" she giggled.

"I'd love to be at that wrap party, wouldn't you?" grinned Matt. "I mean just to watch her in action. Cat going for the flirt of her life!"

"Well, us ordinary mortals don't get invited to flashy parties like that though, do we?" Anna smiled up at her boyfriend. "Though I know Sonja tried to get Cat to wangle an invite for everyone!"

"But no luck?"

"No luck," laughed Anna. "So... while Cat's living it up tomorrow night, what will *we* get up to? Pizza and a video?"

"Hey, I think we can do much better than that!" said Matt, his eyes suddenly lighting up.

"What's that then?" asked Anna.

"Well, Cat's got her flash party, so I think the rest of us saddos who didn't get invited should have our *own* flash party!

"Where?" laughed Anna, trying to work out what was going on in his mind.

"*Your* place!" announced Matt.

"*My* place?" she giggled, thinking of her tiny flat above the End. "You couldn't even have a *normal* party at my place, never mind a *flash* one!"

"You never think big, Anna, that's your trouble," Matt grinned, giving her a hug. "Leave it to me, you'll see..."

Anna could tell by the enthusiastic expression on his face that Matt wasn't about to let her say no.

CHAPTER 18

• •

NOT THE WRAP PARTY

"Hey, Kez, I couldn't believe what Billy was telling me
last night. Astrid's covering for Joe as drummer for
The Loud?" Sonia gave her best friend an earnest look
as they made their way along Station Road on Friday
evening. "He says you're cool about it. Are you, *really*?"

Kerry grimaced. "I don't know about *cool* exactly,
but she was good, Son. And there was nobody else.
You know how much The Loud means to Ollie – it
would fall apart without a drummer."

"What about Ollie? She freaked him out before
didn't she, with her psycho tendencies? I mean,
d'you remember those roses and that Valentine's
picture that she left on his doorstep? If I was Ollie
I'd be dead scared she was just trying to get close to
me again," Sonja said.

"Sonja, don't put weirdo thoughts in my head. I'm trying to stay rational." Kerry put her arm through Sonja's. "We talked it through, on our own – and, although it's a bit bizarre, we decided it was worth a try. She swears she's changed."

"Oh well, I guess she knows we'll all be watching her pretty hard at first," Sonja nodded, giving Kerry's arm a squeeze. "Still, I bet Ollie's going to feel a bit freaked the first time she sits behind him, armed with a pair of drumsticks!"

"You should have seen his face when Astrid admitted she enjoyed drumming because it helped her get rid of all her aggression! I thought he was going to leg it," Kerry giggled. "And the rest of the lads looked pretty fazed too. They were probably thinking – *next time it could be me...* Still, they've told her it's only for a trial period and that Joe takes over whenever he comes home. I'm sure it will be fine..." She trailed off into an uneasy silence.

"What time is it?" Sonja asked, sensing she needed to change the subject. "I forgot to put my watch on after I came out of the shower."

Kerry glanced at her wrist. "Just after nine so the café will be shut now."

"I hope they managed to get everything tidied away early tonight so that everyone can chill out!"

"Well, it was Anna's night off anyway. And

Ollie will have worked like crazy to get everything finished on time – 'specially since there's a party as an incentive!"

"Well, however busy he is, I hope he's going to get changed," said Sonja. "After all, if the rest of us are all going to the bother of getting dressed up for this party – like Matt suggested – then I don't want to sit opposite your boyfriend dressed in his usual scruffy T-shirt and— EEK!"

Sonja gasped and giggled as a warm summer evening breeze blew along the street and lifted up her short, wispy sundress.

"That's the good thing about long straight skirts – they stay put!" laughed Kerry, watching her best friend struggle to keep the pale blue material from drifting upwards and giving the world a glimpse of her knickers.

"You look lovely in that sarong," said Sonja, nodding her head towards her friend's rust and bronze-coloured skirt.

"Thanks. Anyway, what do you think Cat will wear to *her* party tonight?" Kerry wondered.

"It's *got* to be something amazing, hasn't it?" grinned Sonja. "After all, this is her last chance to pull Ben Fitzpatrick!"

"You're right there," nodded Kerry. "But it's a shame she's not coming along to Anna's party tonight. It'll be kind of strange not having her there."

"Do you think she'll care?" Sonja laughed. "She'll be too busy prowling after her precious Ben to think about us for a millisecond."

"Oh, don't be mean, Son!" Kerry said, pulling a face. "It's just that I know Matt suggested this party for a laugh 'cause none of us got invited to the TV do, but I still think it's kind of special. Y'know – it'll be one of the last times we'll all be together before... before..."

Kerry hesitated, her voice suddenly sounding a little hoarse.

"Hey, don't go all soppy on me!" Sonja gently chided her best friend. "Just 'cause me and Joe are leaving Winstead, it doesn't mean the end of everything. We'll all be just as good mates as ever!"

Kerry nodded, but her head was facing down, her long curls hiding her face. Sonja stopped, a couple of metres away from the front door of the End-of-the-Line café, making Kerry pause too.

"And, Kez..." said Sonja.

"What?" Kerry blinked at her.

"Whether we live one street away from each other, or hundreds of miles from each other, we'll *always* be best mates..."

The two girls looked at each other, eyes glistening.

"C'mere, you!" laughed Sonja, pulling Kerry close for a hug.

"You've got to stay in touch, all right?" Kerry gulped, trying her best not to cry.

"Absolutely!" exclaimed Sonja, though the wobble in her voice showed that tears weren't far away either. "You and Ollie will have to come up and stay with me and Owen as often as you can! And Ollie's got e-mail, hasn't he? I'll get an e-mail address and you'll be able to tell me how your teacher training course is going, and how annoying my darling cousin's being, and everything!"

Kerry nodded, her voice lost for a second.

"Hey, what are we wasting time out here for," Sonja suddenly announced, "when there's a party about to start?!"

Right on cue, they heard music drifting over from behind the café.

"C'mon!" grinned Sonja, turning into the alley that ran between the second-hand record shop and the End-of-the-Line café. At the end of it, she pushed open the green wooden door that led into the back yard of the café.

"Wow!" Sonja exclaimed, staring at the long table – surrounded by chairs – in the middle of the yard. In place of a tablecloth, it was draped in vivid red and gold sari material, with loads of flickering night-light candles in clear glass jars dotted down the middle of it.

"Oh, Ollie!" gasped Kerry as she followed behind Sonja and stared up.

"Good, isn't it?" beamed Ollie from his perch atop a stepladder, where he was securing the last of a string of coloured lights to the telephone pole.

At his feet, holding the ladder steady, was Billy, while a little further away Matt was busy positioning a speaker.

"Hi, guys!" Matt called out.

"This is beautiful!" sighed Sonja, leaning her head back and gazing at the canopy of bulbs strung this way and that above their heads, and wrapped all the way up the metal staircase to Anna's front door.

"You wouldn't think it was the same scrappy little yard, would you?" Matt commented.

"Mainly 'cause I was here all day sorting it out!" Ollie pointed out. "As *well* as making tons of food for tonight, as *well* as feeding the normal customers!"

"Round of applause for Ollie!" Billy joked, slapping his hands together. Sonja, Kerry and Matt joined in, giggling as Ollie took a bow at the top of the stepladder.

"And a wolf whistle too for you boys – look at you!" laughed Sonja, taking in the highly unusual sight of Ollie and Billy in smart, short-sleeve shirts. But the compliment was mainly aimed at Matt, who was wearing a trendy black suit with a wide-lapelled Cuban print shirt underneath.

Matt did a twirl then stopped with a hand under his chin, striking a catalogue model pose. "Not too shabby, is it?" he grinned. "And may I just say you girls are looking pretty gorgeous yourselves."

"Thanks, Matt!" Kerry giggled. "So where's Anna?"

"Just getting herself gorgeous too," Matt replied, nodding his head towards the open front door at the top of the stairs. "She'll be down in a second."

At that moment, Nick and Cyndi stepped out of the kitchen doorway. "Hi, girls!" said Nick cheerfully. "Hey, Matt – we're off now. Anna's got the spare keys to lock this place up once you're finished with the kitchen."

"Thanks, Nick!" Matt grinned, giving Nick the thumbs-up. "And thanks again for letting us use the yard and everything!"

"No problem. I got this dump of a yard tidied for nothing, didn't I?" the café owner laughed.

"Oh, honey!" exclaimed Cyndi, suddenly. "Don't you look pretty!"

Everyone in the yard turn to stare as Anna came down the metal steps from the flat. Her long brown hair hung loose and silky smooth down her back.

Her dress – a knee-length, baby-blue, silky halter-neck – showed off the creamy skin of her well-toned arms and legs.

"Thanks, Cyndi," said Anna shyly, suddenly self-conscious with everyone's eyes glued to her.

"Wooh-hoo!" Matt called out appreciatively, moving towards the staircase and holding his hand out to help her down.

"Look how pretty your hair is, now you haven't got it all scraped back like you usually do!" cooed Cyndi, clasping her hands in front of her chest. "Oh, an' that reminds me – Anna, honey, can I ask a favour?"

"Of course!" said Anna, swapping a quick glance with Matt that said 'maybe things *aren't* so bad? Maybe I *could* get on with Cyndi?'

"Well," said Cyndi, putting on a puppy dog expression, "can you just make sure you're on time in the morning because I'm not gonna be around to look after things – I made an appointment at the hairdresser's first thing and Nick's out too, aren't you, sugar-pie?"

Matt watched as Anna's shoulders sagged.

"Yes, no problem..." Anna replied, mustering a limp smile, but inside she was seething. *How dare she? I'm never late to work in the morning! How does she think we managed before? Well, she can stuff her badge and her cheesy photos. I've had enough!*

CHAPTER 19

● ●

FLIRTING – TAKE FOUR AND CUT!

"How do I look? Marks out of ten?"

Cat twisted and turned in front of the mirror in the posh Balinard Hotel loos, with Vikki standing beside her.

"It's got to be a perfect ten," said Vikki, standing back as far as she could, just to take in the spectacle of Cat's outfit. Or maybe it was to get away from the glare...

Cat was out to shine. And there was no arguing that she was going to shimmy and shine in her gold halter-neck top, gold low-slung trousers, gold chain belt hanging loose around her hips and gold high sandals. Even the tips of her fingernails were gold and, when she moved, the metallic powder she'd dusted across her shoulders and cheekbones shimmered in the light.

Smiling with anticipation, Cat thought back with a delicious shiver to this afternoon, when filming had finally finished. It had been very dry and stuffy in the launderette, under all the spotlights – as Cat had noticed the day before. Today she'd been ready. It had nothing to do with luck that Cat had been on hand with a bottle of sparkling mineral water as Ben strode away from the set, complaining that his mouth felt like sandpaper.

Cat had been rewarded with one of Ben's very best smiles as she'd presented him with a brimming plastic glassful. "You saved my life – again!" he'd said. "How come you're always in the right place at the right time?"

"I've been learning so much all week," Cat had told him, pleased at how natural and professional she sounded. "It's the details that are important, right?"

"Right!" Ben had laughed. "You're a natural, darling. Hope you've been invited to the wrap party tonight."

"Oh yes – I'll be there!" Cat had beamed. Ben had handed back the cup and their fingers had brushed.

"See you later, Cat," he'd called back over his shoulder.

"It's *Pat*," she'd corrected, then slapped her hand across her mouth when she'd realised what she'd said. But it didn't matter. Ben hadn't seem to notice...

"He's certainly going to notice you in *that!*" Vikki declared, bringing Cat back to the present.

"*Who'll* notice me?" asked Cat, playing the innocent as she patted the tight blonde knots of hair she'd twisted up on either side of her head.

"Ben, of course!" laughed Vikki. "Who did you think I meant – Santa Claus?"

"I'm not dressing up for *him* – I'm dressing up for *me!*" trilled Cat, though she wasn't fooling anyone.

"Well, whoever you've dressed for, are you ready to go and find this party?" asked Vikki.

"Of course!" Cat replied, with a force ten smile, bright enough to match her outfit.

The two girls left the loos, which they'd darted into as soon as the taxi had dropped them off at the Balinard Hotel. Their high shoes sinking into the plush carpeting, Cat and Vikki aimed for the snooty-looking bloke at the desk.

"Hi!" smiled Cat.

The desk clerk continued doodling something on a pad on the counter. Cat and Vikki exchanged glances. Obviously neither of them looked posh enough for the Balinard Hotel – well, at least not in this bloke's view. Just as Cat was about to speak again, the desk clerk finally lifted his head.

"Hello," he replied unsmilingly.

"Can you tell us which function suite the TV party is happening in?" Cat asked him.

"I'm sorry," frowned the guy, "but both our function suites are hosting wedding receptions tonight."

"Look, it's OK!" said Cat, leaning on the counter and giving the unhelpful desk clerk a knowing look. "We *have* been invited! Just ask Daniel Farrow – he's the production assistant, he said it would be all right!"

"Ah, you mean Mr Farrow and his party," the man said haughtily. "Through there – the door on the left."

"Thank you *so* much!" said Cat sarcastically.

"Hey, *he'll* never win any prizes for helpfulness!" whispered Vikki as the two girls followed his directions.

"I felt like pushing that pen of his up his nose!" Cat giggled back. "Snobby gi— oh! This can't be right! This door leads to the bar!"

"Maybe there's a function suite at the back of it!" Vikki suggested, pushing open the door.

"Maybe," shrugged Cat, "but I—" She stood in

the doorway, a vision in twinkling gold. In front of her was a smoky bar – posher than the Railway Tavern or The Swan, but a bar nevertheless. The good news was the fact that the two girls recognised almost everyone there as members of the TV crew; the bad news was, they were all dressed in jeans and trainers, and downing pints.

"I thought this was supposed to be a party!" Cat hissed at Vikki as the room slowly quietened and everyone turned – as if their eyes were drawn by a golden magnet – towards the door.

• • •

"Rubbish party, isn't it?" Cat muttered glumly, her chin resting on her hands, her elbows on her golden knees.

Vikki was sitting beside her on a brown leather sofa in a mainly deserted part of the low-lit room. It was much more crowded over by the bar, where loads of blokes – plus Rhona and Dawn – were all drinking and chattering and laughing.

"Well, I suppose it's more of a booze-up than a party," Vikki replied.

"Why's it called a wrap 'party' then? Why don't they call it a wrap 'booze-up'?" Cat demanded.

"I dunno," Vikki shrugged.

"I'm overdressed, aren't I?" said Cat, pulling at her fancy gold trousers.

"Um... maybe just a little bit," said Vikki, struggling to be supportive. "But who cares?"

"I do!" whined Cat. "And this was all for Ben's benefit!"

Vikki decided it was tactful to say nothing.

"He's not coming, is he?" said Cat mournfully. "I mean, we've been here for nearly two hours!"

"I guess not," Vikki agreed.

"'See you later,' he said, Vik. '*See you later.*' Why did he lie to me?"

"I don't think he did, Cat," Vikki told her. "I think it's just something he says to everyone. Hell – he even said it to me."

When they'd arrived, once everyone had got over the shock of Cat's outfit, Daniel had cheerfully informed them that Ben Fitzpatrick might or might not have time to pop in for ten minutes or so, before he headed back down to London, where his mate was having a party.

"He's mates with Kate Moss!" Cat moaned. "Of course he's going to go to *her* party and not stay around for *this*!"

"But—"

"But nothing, Vik!" sighed Cat. "This has been a *total* waste of time!"

"Maybe it's been a waste of time when it comes to you trying to snog Ben Fitzpatrick," conceded Vikki. "But listen, Cat – stuff him. Don't you think what I was just saying earlier is much more exciting?"

"Tell me again," moped Cat, fixing her gaze on the chattering TV technicians once more. "I wasn't really listening."

"I knew it! Anyway, I was speaking to Jon, the director, and *he* told me he's been very impressed with the work me and you have done this week!"

"Big wow..." said Cat flatly.

"But it *is* amazing, Cat!" continued Vikki. "I mean, we thought he was this snooty director who didn't even know we existed, and now he's gone to the bother of giving me some acting agency contacts for us both in London!"

The news didn't get the response Vikki hoped for. Cat had sunk her head into her hands and was groaning gently. "How can I face my friends again after this?" she mumbled. "I told them all that tonight was the night for me and Ben!"

"But why are you even bothered about him, Cat? So what if he's appeared in *OK* magazine? I don't think much of someone who can't even turn up for a quick drink with the people he's been working with all week!"

"*And* he's short!" Cat said bitterly, her face still buried in her hands.

"*And* he's short," Vikki agreed with her. "Cat, you deserve a much nicer – and taller – bloke than him."

Slowly, Cat raised her head and turned to face her friend again. "I do, don't I?" she repeated, a worrying glint appearing in her eyes.

"Uh, yes, definitely!" nodded Vikki, sensing that Cat had just formulated a new plan.

"How do I look?" Cat asked, straightening herself up and wiping a finger under each eye. One of her tight knots of hair had slipped slightly to the side and started to unravel, but Vikki didn't bother to point it out.

"You look great," she said simply and, with that, Cat clattered up from her seat and twinkled into action.

• • •

"Cat! I was just coming over to speak to you!" exclaimed Daniel, tearing himself away from the cameraman he was chatting to.

For the first time, Cat noticed that his eyes were like a lion's – golden-brown. They practically matched what she was wearing. *It's an omen...* she decided to herself.

"I'm so glad to get you alone," said Daniel, turning away from the nearest crew members for privacy.

"Are you?" asked Cat, arching her eyebrows. This was it. She couldn't believe she'd got it so wrong. She'd wasted all her flirting efforts on someone who didn't deserve it. But he wasn't here, and Daniel most definitely was. And Daniel had been so cool to her all week – how could she have been so blind?

It's not too late... she decided, giving Daniel her best killer Cat stare.

"Cat," said Daniel softly, reaching for her hand.

Cat held her breath, letting her fingers curl round his.

"There's something I need to ask you..."

She looked into his golden-brown eyes and couldn't wait to hear what was coming next...

CHAPTER 20

● ●

HAPPY ENDINGS

The night was dark and star-spangled, though it was hard to see the stars twinkle at all, with the bright lights bobbing gently above yard where the night-lights flickered low.

Around the table sat Kerry and Ollie, Joe and Meg, Sonja, Andy and Matt. For the moment, there was no sign of Billy or Gabrielle – who'd been invited at Billy's request – or of Anna. Billy and Gaby had disappeared inside the End's kitchen, supposedly to make coffee for everyone, but they were certainly taking their time about it.

Matt, sitting at one end of the table, glanced up at the flat and wondered where Anna had got to. She'd disappeared upstairs to switch CDs a little while ago, but although the music had changed, she still hadn't come back down yet.

"Smile!" Maya ordered her friends, standing a couple of steps up on the metal staircase and pointing her camera at them.

"Hey!" Ollie called out as soon as the flash had gone off. "Pity you've already entered a photo for that big competition. Maya. 'Cause with our gorgeous faces in it, this shot would have got you first place, *easy*!"

"With *your* face in it, Ol, it's lucky the *lens* didn't crack!" Sonja teased back at him.

Maya lowered the camera and walked back to her seat, smiling as her friends fooled around. She hadn't the heart to tell them her news and bring the mood of the party down. If they knew that Alex had left a message on the Joshis' answering machine earlier, telling her that she *hadn't* been placed in the competition, they'd all have felt sorry for her. Maya – practical as always – hadn't really expected to come anywhere in such a big competition, although it would have been great if she had. All that mattered to her now was her determination to make photography her career – whatever her parents had to say about it.

"Listen, I think I'll go and see what's happened to our lovely hostess," Matt joked, getting to his feet.

"And tell her to hurry!" Sonja called after him. "She promised to bring down her tarot cards and do me a reading!"

"Hey, I can tell your future for you, if you want!" said Ollie with a cheeky grin.

"Oh, yeah?" Sonja replied, arching one eyebrow and gazing at him suspiciously.

Wafting his fork in the air, Ollie closed his eyes and tried to look mystical.

"Ah, yes... something will be missing from your life... that bit of cheesecake!" And in a microsecond, Ollie had stabbed the last piece of pudding Sonja had been toying with on her plate and stuffed it in his mouth.

"Ollie, you pig!" Sonja shrieked.

"Yep. That's it – I'm officially stuffed!" said Ollie, through a mouthful of food and patting his belly. "I don't know if I've got room for any more beer!"

"I'll bet you'll manage though!" giggled Kerry as female vocals drifted through the speakers, siphoned down from Anna's flat.

"So," said Sonja, giving Ollie a withering look and turning to Meg, "not long till Brighton. Not long till you and Joe are together!"

"Well, give or take an hour and a half's drive on the motorway!" said Joe, more exactly.

"Yes, but think of it this way," said Meg, snuggling closer to her boyfriend, "every weekend, I'll be with you in your trendy flat in Shoreditch—"

Joe laughed at the thought of his paint-peeling new flat being described as trendy.

"—or you'll be down in Brighton with me, talking moonlit walks along the beach!"

"Sounds good to me..." said Joe, moving closer to kiss her.

"Awww!" The others howled in unison around the table. Joe and Meg jumped apart at the sudden noise.

"C'mon, since this is supposed to be a posh dinner party," said Ollie, pausing to burp as the others groaned, "let's have a toast – to our soon-to-depart ace drummer and all-round top bloke!"

"To Joe!" said the others, raising their drinks.

"Speech!" called out Andy, laughing at the sight of Joe's embarrassed face.

"No– I... no, it's—" bumbled Joe, hating being the centre of attention. Meg giggled at his side.

"Come on, Joe!" said Matt, thumping him on the shoulder. "Say a few words, mate!"

Joe coughed, then his eyes settled on one of the others round the table. Inspiration struck...

"I want to make a toast..." he began, holding his glass in the air.

"Yeah! Go on then!" Ollie encouraged him.

"I want to make a toast to... Kerry!"

Kerry's mouth dropped open.

"Me?!" she exclaimed, looking as embarrassed as Joe had done seconds before.

"Yep – a toast to Kerry for being so cool," Joe continued, "that she's letting Astrid take my place in the band!"

"Yeah – cheers for being OK about Stalker Girl coming on board!" said Andy cheerfully. "Or we'd have had to end up using a drum machine. And even I can see she's a bit sexier than one of those!"

"Oh, don't call her Stalker Girl!" winced Kerry. "I might change my mind! And she says she's changed, so you've got to give her a break."

"Joe's right – you are so brilliant!" said Ollie proudly, grabbing her by the hand and pulling her close to him. "Do you know that?"

"I'm not brilliant – I'm just trying to be fair!" Kerry shrugged, still feeling awkward.

"And remember, lads, when we tell Astrid she's got the gig, we have to spell it out to her that it's only temporary, while Joe's away at uni," Ollie added, glancing over at the boys.

Joe could see his speech had embarrassed Kerry and decided to change the subject. "Anyone else got anything we can celebrate?" he asked, holding his glass aloft and looking round the table.

"Nope – but what about a drink to commiserate?" A vision in gold stood at the alleyway gate.

"Cat!" exclaimed Sonja. "What are you doing here?"

"She's decided that we went to the wrong party," Vikki boomed from behind her, ushering a dejected-looking Cat into the fairy-lit yard. "So, is there room for two more round that table?"

• • •

Matt paused in the open doorway and saw Anna sitting cross-legged on the floor of her living room, her tarot cards spread out in front of her on the coffee table.

"What are they telling you now?" he said softly, walking towards her.

"I don't know exactly..." she sighed. "I don't think I know what the future holds, but I'm not sure I can stay here, Matt."

"Well, let's see if *I* can read them," he said, flopping down on to the floor beside her. "Now *this* one says to me that you should cheer up, 'cause you're going on holiday with your fantastic boyfriend soon!"

"Oh, Matt, I know you're trying to be sweet, but I need more than just a holiday," Anna sighed again. "I mean, I know I didn't plan on waitressing forever, but at the moment I feel like a skivvy! The only thing that's stopping me chucking it all in is that I don't know what I would do next or where I would go..."

"C'mere..." ordered Matt, clambering to his feet again and pulling her with him. "These cards are rubbish. If you want to know the future, you've got to look at the stars..."

"But, Matt!" protested Anna as he dragged her towards the living room window.

"Ah, be quiet," he told her. "You wanted to look at the stars at New Year, remember? Now it's your turn to look and then listen to Mystic Matt."

Anna giggled and looked up at the stars he was now pointing to.

"See that constellation over there? The one that looks like a coat hanger?"

"No," Anna giggled again.

"Good. Anyway, that constellation tells me your future," he proclaimed, giving her waist a squeeze.

"Oh, yes? And what does it say?" she smiled, playing along.

"It says you won't be a waitress forever – you're going to find your true vocation soon."

"And what's that going to be?"

"I don't know, do I? That's up to you. Anyway, shut up; I'm not finished."

"Go on then, what else does the cosmic coat

hanger have in store for me?"

"Travel," Matt nodded earnestly.

"Yeah, yeah, the holiday to Ibiza," Anna shrugged.

"No – it's more complicated than that," said Matt, his eyes still glued to the heavens.

"Oh, yes?" Anna replied.

"Yep. It's saying that you and me are going to be busy on this holiday. We're going to make contacts – lots of them. And we're going to sort out work for ourselves for the whole of next season. We're going to spend the whole summer together out there in the sunshine... maybe longer depending on how it goes."

"But, Matt," gasped Anna, not quite able to take in the significance of what he was saying.

"And OK, so you might have to waitress for a while out there, but it'll be a lot more fun than here *and* it'll give you plenty of time to think about what you want to do next, like studying or whatever..."

At last, he turned away from the night sky and looked into Anna's face, wondering what her reaction was to his words.

"Matt... I... that would be perfect!" she whispered.

Matt slid both his arms around her and pulled her close. "Anna, it's me and you, all the way, from now on," he muttered, holding her tightly.

For a few minutes they stayed that way, aware only of the happiness cocooning them both.

"Hey, listen!" said Anna, suddenly pulling away from him. "Isn't that Cat's voice?"

Matt tilted his head to one side and heard roars of laughter coming from the yard – with Cat's voice booming loudly over the top of it all.

"What's *she* doing here? What's happened to that fancy-pants party of hers?" he frowned.

"Come on then, let's see what's going on!"

Hand in hand, they hurried towards the doorway and out on to the metal verandah at the top of the stairs.

"Hey, you two, come on down!" Sonja called up to them. "You've got to hear this stuff!"

Anna led the way, clattering down the steps – past Billy and Gaby standing at the kitchen door, fingers, Anna noticed, entwined – and grabbed the nearest chair.

"What's happened to your party, Cat?" she asked as Matt flopped down next to her.

Cat was sitting at the end of the table, the gold of her outfit making her look like a person-shaped glitterball in the candlelight.

"Oh, you haven't missed out on much," Cat shrugged, sending twinkles of light reverberating around the walls of the yard. "Only me, making a fool of myself over a boy! Again!"

She rolled her eyes and slumped theatrically in her seat. Clearly, she hadn't had the best of nights, but to Anna and Matt it was also obvious that Cat was now loving being the centre of attention as she relayed her sob story.

"Wait till you hear this!" Sonja giggled. "It's the best! Ben Fitzpatrick never turned up at the party tonight so Cat *only* tried to flirt with that Daniel guy instead, and Daniel *only* went and—"

"Thank you, Sonja, I'm perfectly capable of telling my own story!" Cat snapped at her cousin.

"Go on then," grinned Matt. "Tell us!"

"Well, like I just told the others," Cat began, ignoring the fact that Andy was groaning and had his hands covering his face, "*I* start flirting with Daniel and *he* starts getting very flirty back. Or so I think."

"And?" asked Anna, wondering what the others were all snickering at and what was up with Andy.

"And so the next thing, Daniel says he's got something to ask me," Cat continued, one of her blonde knots of hair now unfurling into a tangled ponytail on the side of her head.

"Which was?" Anna prompted as the sniggering all around the table reached epic proportions.

"Which was..." said Cat, dragging her story out for dramatic effect, "is Andy seeing anyone?"

"You mean..." gasped Anna.

"Yep," said Cat, nodding. "He fancies *him* and not *me!*"

"Oh, I'm sorry, Cat!" Andy blushed. "I sussed as much on Thursday, but..."

"Anyway," Cat interrupted, rifling around in her bag and pulling out a piece of paper, "Andy, this is for you – Daniel's mobile number – if you want it."

Andy reached out to take it from her – but Cat snatched it back. "Ah, ah, *ah!*" she told him off. "I think you owe me a big fat kiss for that one!" Cat grinned at him, pointing to her cheek with her finger.

Andy grinned back, leant over the now-empty plates of food and landed a smacker on her face.

"Well," smirked Cat, passing him the paper, "I don't know if it really counts, but at least I got *one* kiss off a bloke tonight!"

"So the whole party was a waste of time then?" Kerry piped up.

"Don't get her started on that again, *please!*" Vikki rolled her eyes.

"No – I'm *not* going to moan about that any more!" Cat announced. "And anyway, it's helped me see that maybe I've been getting it all wrong. Maybe acting isn't really for me after all."

"Oh, yeah?" frowned Sonja. "Why not?"

Every one of her friends around the table silently

wondered if Cat had finally seen sense. Cat was a great actress – and didn't they all know that, on a day-to-day basis, as well as what they'd seen her do on the stage – but they all suspected that what she really wanted was *fame*. Nothing would stop Cat from having stars in her eyes.

"Well, it's just not... *glamorous* enough!" shrugged Cat, a little dusting of gold make-up shaking off her as she did so. "No, I think I should maybe think about a *new* career!"

"As what?" barked Matt, a smile splitting his face.

"Well, to*night*, Matthew, I'm going to be... a singer. Tra-la!"

"What?" squawked half her friends around the table as the others sat open-mouthed.

"Well, I sang when I did that panto at college, didn't I?" said Cat defensively. "So I've got an OK start. I just need to take a few more singing lessons for technique, and work on my image, and I could be out there – being the next... I dunno – Kylie or Madonna even!"

It wasn't Kylie or Madonna wafting out of the speakers at that moment, but that didn't stop Cat. Before anyone could make any comment, she leapt to her feet, clambered up on her chair and began singing along at the top of her voice.

Ollie looked across the table at Anna and Matt

and behind them at Billy and Gaby. "Whoo-hooh!" he called out encouragingly and started clapping his hands. Soon they, and everyone else, joined in as Cat threw her arms out and gave it all she'd got.

Maya raised her camera and, as she caught Cat in action, she spotted lights going on in the upstairs flat next door, where Nick and Cyndi must have been disturbed from their romantic night in by Cat's caterwauling.

"She's not bad!" Kerry giggled in Ollie's ear as she clapped along.

"She's not good either!" Ollie laughed back. "But with Cat, I'd never say never. She's the one out of all of us who could be a star – she wants it badly enough!"

Kerry gazed at her boyfriend's face then around her, at all her friends.

Maybe, way in the future, Cat will end up with a hit record, or starring with Tom Cruise in some blockbuster, she decided. *But this is what makes me happy – being with my best mates, right now.*

And, with that, Kerry kicked off her shoes, clambered on to her seat and surprised everyone – including herself – by singing along with Cat.

CAN YOU KEEP A SECRET?

• •

Do you think that keeping a secret is delicious – or too much like hard work? Are you the type who'll open your mouth and spill straight away, or can you be trusted to keep those lips zipped tight shut? Try our quiz and find out...

---

1. Your drama teacher tells you that you've got the lead in the school play, but asks you to keep it quiet till he's told the other girl who was up for it. You spend the rest of break...

a) In a huddle with your mates, telling them your amazing news.
b) Chewing your fingernails, waiting impatiently until you can let people know.

---

2. A friend admits that she's got a thing for this obnoxious loser of a boy you both know. She begs you not to tell anyone else. You swear you won't...

a) But you know you will. It's just too freaky to keep to yourself!
b) 'Cause you can see how mortified she is, and – hey – everyone's allowed to make a mistake!

3. **A boyfriend once confessed that he's got a phobia... about ladybirds. You promised never to breathe a word – except now you've split up and you're dying to tell your girlfriends...**

a) And why not? It's not like you owe him any loyalty if you're not dating him any more!

b) But you don't. He told you that secret in confidence, and just 'cause you're not an item any more, doesn't mean you should break that trust.

---

4. **Your friend tells her parents that she's been out with you, when really she's been seeing a boy they disapprove of. You run into her dad next day, and he if asks if you two had fun. You...**

a) Say straight off that she wasn't with you. You can't handle getting into some big complicated lie.

b) Shrug and say something non-commital, then corner your mate and tell her that she'd better sort it out – it's not fair to involve you in secrets like that.

---

5. **You're looking for something in a cupboard when you find a plastic bag full of goodies. It's your birthday next week, so this stuff's obviously meant for you. Do you...**

a) Brandish the bag at your mum and say, "You didn't hide this very well, did you!"

b) Keep schtum, and act dutifully surprised when you tear off the wrapping paper on your big day.

6. **People are bitching about your best mate, saying she's gone sulky and moody. You know it's because her parents are splitting up, but she wants to keep it to herself right now. Next time you catch someone having a go, you...**

a) Can't hold it in any longer. You've got to set people straight and put an end to the moaning.

b) Say nothing, but advise your best mate to get it out in the open so the rest of her friends can be understanding too.

7. **A friend is driving you all nuts, so you organise a night out without her, just this once. But during the day, she gets you on your own and asks if there's something going on. You look her straight in the eye and...**

a) Tell her yes; you're all going out, and she's not invited, simple as that.

b) Tell her no, 'cause you don't want to hurt her feelings. But you realise that you and your other friends have got to sort out the problem properly.

8. **Your sister has 'borrowed' a fiver from your mum's purse, and says she's going to put it back when she gets paid from her Saturday job. Then you see your mum checking her purse, looking concerned. You...**

a) Put your mum out of her misery straightaway and point the finger at your sister.

b) Get hold of your sister and lay a serious guilt trip on her about how stressed out she's made your mum. She'd better fix it, or else you're telling.

9. **Your gran has won a chunk of money on the Lottery. She's buying everyone in the family a present, but has asked you not to tell anyone else about her win. You...**

a) Immediately tell all your friends – well, they don't really count, do they? And how else can you explain your new personal CD player?

b) Don't really understand why your gran wants to keep her good news secret, but she *is* your gran, so of course you won't blab.

10. **You've just been asked out by the coolest guy around. Your head's spinning and you feel like yelling out your news for the world to hear. Instead you...**

a) Restrict yourself to phoning up *every* friend in your address book and letting them know who's a lucky girl!

b) Tell only your best friend – for now. After all, if the date doesn't work out, there'll be less explaining to do.

NOW CHECK OUT HOW YOU SCORED...

SO, CAN YOU KEEP A SECRET?

• •

Mostly a

Keep a secret? You couldn't – not even if you were offered a million pounds and a hot date with all of Five! Admittedly, some secrets can be a bit dodgy (see questions 4 and 8), but on the whole, when you hear a secret, you tend to see it as an excellent piece of gossip and don't really think of the consequences, like making a fool of the person who told you the secret in the first place! Here's a tip: next time you hear something juicy, try keeping it to yourself for a day before you decide whether or not to share it around. Give your conscience a chance to work, before your mouth gets you – and other people – in trouble!

Mostly b

Anyone would be glad to have a friend like you. You're loyal, trustworthy and thoughtful – and you sure know how to keep a secret. Be proud of your self-control in the face of excellent gossipworthy material! But there's one thing you should remember – not all secrets are good. If keeping a secret means covering up for someone else's bad behaviour (see questions 4 and 8) then you really should think twice before you get involved and land yourself in an uncomfortable situation. Keeping quiet isn't always the right thing to do!